P9-BYM-887

The moment was so magical that Kirsten was afraid to breathe for fear it was all a dream and she'd wake up alone in her bed, her arms wrapped around her pillow.

She was spellbound by his heady scent, by the warmth of his breath and the heat of his touch.

As the kiss deepened and their lips parted, his tongue brushed hers, making her knees go weak. So she reached for his waist to steady herself. As she did so, he slipped his arms around her, drawing her close, kissing her until she was tempted to drag him inside and see what happened next.

Oh, lordy. If this was the way Jeremy kissed a woman good-night, she wondered what it would be like to welcome him into her bed, into her…life.

Dear Reader,

It's February in Red Rock, Texas, and love is in the air. Even the shops and stores downtown and in nearby San Antonio have gotten into the Valentine's Day spirit by decorating with hearts and flowers.

This month is also the perfect time to read a romance, so I'm glad you chose *Healing Dr. Fortune,* the second book in The Fortunes of Texas: Lost…and Found.

In this story, you'll meet Kirsten Allen, who has a lot on her plate these days, including an unemployed brother who needs a helping hand and a baby nephew who needs a mother's touch. But when she runs into Dr. Jeremy Fortune, who is waiting in Red Rock until his missing father is found, sparks fly and love blossoms.

So find a cozy spot and curl up with a little Texas romance.

Happy reading!

Judy

HEALING
DR. FORTUNE

JUDY DUARTE

Silhouette®

SPECIAL EDITION®

Published by Silhouette Books

America's Publisher of Contemporary Romance

If you purchased this book without a cover you should be aware that this book is stolen property. It was reported as "unsold and destroyed" to the publisher, and neither the author nor the publisher has received any payment for this "stripped book."

Special thanks and acknowledgment to Judy Duarte for her contribution to the Fortunes of Texas: Lost...and Found miniseries.

SILHOUETTE BOOKS

ISBN-13: 978-0-373-65578-6

Recycling programs
for this product may
not exist in your area.

HEALING DR. FORTUNE

Copyright © 2011 by Harlequin Books S.A.

All rights reserved. Except for use in any review, the reproduction or utilization of this work in whole or in part in any form by any electronic, mechanical or other means, now known or hereafter invented, including xerography, photocopying and recording, or in any information storage or retrieval system, is forbidden without the written permission of the editorial office, Silhouette Books, 233 Broadway, New York, NY 10279 U.S.A.

This is a work of fiction. Names, characters, places and incidents are either the product of the author's imagination or are used fictitiously, and any resemblance to actual persons, living or dead, business establishments, events or locales is entirely coincidental.

This edition published by arrangement with Harlequin Books S.A.

For questions and comments about the quality of this book please contact us at Customer_eCare@Harlequin.ca.

® and TM are trademarks of Harlequin Books S.A., used under license. Trademarks indicated with ® are registered in the United States Patent and Trademark Office, the Canadian Trade Marks Office and in other countries.

Visit Silhouette Books at www.eHarlequin.com

Printed in U.S.A.

Books by Judy Duarte

JUDY DUARTE

always knew there was a book inside her, but since English was her least favorite subject in school, she never considered herself a writer. An avid reader who enjoys a happy ending, Judy couldn't shake the dream of creating a book of her own.

Her dream became a reality in March of 2002, when Silhouette Special Edition released her first book, *Cowboy Courage*. Since then, she has published more than twenty novels. In July of 2005, Judy won the prestigious Readers' Choice Award for *The Rich Man's Son*.

Judy makes her home near the beach in Southern California.

In memory of
Lydia Bustos, the sister I never had,
the friend I'll never forget.
My loss is Heaven's gain.

Chapter One

Dr. Jeremy Fortune stepped out the front door of the Red Rock Medical Center and headed for the parking lot, his mood dark as the storm clouds that gathered overhead.

It had been over a month since his father had disappeared on what would have been the older man's wedding day, and in spite of all the efforts to find him, there'd been very few leads and the trail had gone cold.

William Fortune had been involved in a car accident that took place a hundred miles from the Red Rock church in which he was to be wed. The other driver, a young woman, had died upon impact. But for days, authorities hadn't realized a second vehicle had been involved until they spotted William's silver Mercedes, which had plummeted down an embankment and into a deeply wooded area, where it had been partially hidden by brush and rocks.

There hadn't been any sign of William, though—no blood and no indication that he'd been injured or…worse. It was as if he'd vanished without a trace.

A photograph of Molly, his first wife, had been found tucked into his visor, which had led some of the tabloids to report that he'd been running away. But Jeremy knew better than that.

William Fortune had been eagerly awaiting the ceremony that would unite him in holy matrimony to Lily, the widow of his cousin Ryan. And he'd been looking forward to spending the rest of his life with the woman he'd recently come to love and respect. Besides, his family and his close friends were important to him, and he wouldn't have left without telling any of them. Not of his own accord, anyway.

At first, Jeremy had feared that his father had been kidnapped, but there were no ransom notes found, no phone calls demanding money.

So where was he?

As a driven and dedicated orthopedic surgeon, Jeremy relied on logic and reason to solve problems, which he always faced head-on. But there wasn't anything logical about his father's disappearance.

Jeremy didn't usually trust feelings or hunches, but he couldn't shake the belief that his father was still alive and out there—*somewhere.*

Maybe that was because Jeremy had lost too many

family members already and wasn't going to accept the possibility that he might have lost another.

Nevertheless, he wouldn't leave Texas and return to California until his father was found—one way or another. So he'd taken a leave of absence from his medical practice in Sacramento, which didn't seem to bother him nearly as much as he'd thought it would.

He suspected that had something to do with the fact that, even before coming to Red Rock for his father's wedding, he'd been reevaluating his life choices. And he hoped that a little distance would help him sort it all out.

Still, to keep himself busy during the day and to make himself useful, he'd been volunteering his time at the Red Rock Medical Center, which the Fortune Foundation helped fund. And today was no different.

He glanced at his wristwatch. It was just past four-thirty and a little too early to head for the restaurant. He was meeting his brother and new sister-in-law for dinner at Red tonight—his favorite local restaurant—and he didn't want to drive all the way back to the Double Crown Ranch, where he'd been staying.

Maybe he ought to use the extra time to stop by the bookstore and pick up a couple novels before meeting Drew and Deanna. He'd been battling insomnia lately, so he'd been doing a lot of reading.

As his shoes crunched along the gritty, leaf- and twig-littered sidewalk, a somber mood continued to weigh him down, which seemed to happen whenever his mind wasn't on his work and his patients.

Oddly enough, it had lifted last night—during a dream of all things. He wasn't one to give nocturnal fantasies much thought, but this one had been especially unusual—and real.

The scene had come upon him during the wee hours, but in his mind's eye, the afternoon sun had cast a golden glow upon a tree-lined street much like some of those that could be found in the nicer neighborhoods in Red Rock.

He'd pulled into the driveway of a two-story home, which had been freshly painted—white, with green and black trim. The lawn was lush and neatly mowed, the plants and shrubs well manicured. A petite woman sat in a wicker rocking chair on the front porch, near a black window box that was chock-full of brightly colored flowers.

It was, he decided, a typical Norman Rockwell scene, and his heart soared upon envisioning it.

He'd tried to get a glimpse of the woman's face, but she was looking down at a pink-flannel-wrapped bundle in her arms, her honey-brown hair hanging in a soft tumble of curls that blocked his view.

"I'm home," he'd said, as he'd climbed from the car and shut the door. Then he'd hurried up the side-walk to greet the mother and child, his steps light. The somber mood that had been plaguing him recently had disappeared completely, leaving him happier and more contented than he'd remembered being in a long, long time.

As the woman turned to face him, so he would finally

be able to get a good glimpse of her, the dream had suddenly ended, transporting him from the springtime to winter, from day to night.

He knew that the subconscious did crazy things while the mind and body slept, yet for a brief moment, he'd felt whole and…alive. And when he awoke, he realized what he'd been missing in his outwardly successful life—a wife and a family of his own.

Too bad he couldn't put a name and a face to the woman he'd imagined in his dream. But it really didn't matter. Her image had been merely symbolic, a sign of what he'd been lacking.

As he neared the parking space where he'd left his car earlier in the day, he heard footsteps behind him and glanced over his shoulder to see a petite woman approaching. She wore a pair of slender-fit denim jeans, a snug white T-shirt and a pink jacket to ward off the chill. In her arms, she held a baby wrapped in a blue shawl. She was studying the child, so he couldn't quite see her face.

But damn… With hair the shade of golden honey, she could at least pass for the woman in his dream.

If he were the kind of guy to believe in premonitions, he just might wonder if she was a walking, talking dream come true.

He wasn't, though. But he turned around just the same, drawn to her for some other reason he'd yet to figure out.

As she looked up and spotted him, her lips parted and her steps slowed. She had the face of a magazine cover girl, delicate features and expressive blue eyes with thick, dark lashes.

"Excuse me," she said, adjusting the strap of the diaper bag that hung on her shoulder. "Are you a doctor?"

Jeremy, who was still wearing a lab coat over his street clothes, punctuated a nod by saying, "Yes, I am."

"Oh, good. I was hoping to have the baby examined, and I wondered if…if you could take a look at him."

"I'm not a pediatrician," Jeremy said. "I'm an orthopedic surgeon. The clinic is still open, though. I'm sure someone will be able to see him today."

She glanced over her shoulder, then to the right and the left. "I can't wait. And I'm worried about the baby. I just want to make sure that he's okay."

"What seems to be the problem?" he asked. Did the child have a fever or any particular symptoms?

"Nothing really, I suppose." She looked at the little guy in her arms, then back to Jeremy. "I just want to make sure he's healthy."

That was odd, he thought. But he eased closer to look at the baby, who appeared to be about two months old. On the upside, his eyes were bright and alert, his cheeks were plump and his little arms were filled out. There was no obvious reason to suspect he was sick or had been neglected.

Jeremy looked back at the mother, who seemed a little fidgety. "Like I said, I'm not a pediatrician. And without an actual exam, it's hard to say for sure. But I don't see anything that would make me think that he isn't healthy."

Her nervous expression melted into one of relief. "Oh, thank goodness."

Jeremy wasn't sure why she was so anxious, why she wouldn't go inside and join the other patients waiting to be seen.

"Just as a side note," he added, "the services of the clinic are free for those who can't—"

"Thank you, but it's not that. I was already inside. I waited for more than an hour, and there were still several people in front of me. But I really need to get home."

To a husband, he suspected. And he couldn't help feeling a bit disappointed by the realization.

Of course, he wasn't going to put much stock in a crazy dream and a chance meeting with a woman who bore a slight resemblance to the one he'd envisioned last night. But it wouldn't hurt to check the baby for bumps and bruises.

He reached out to stroke the child's cheek, and the little one grabbed his finger, latching on tight and causing his heart to flip-flop. What was *that* reaction all about?

The woman glanced at her wristwatch, and her breath caught. "I'm sorry. I really need to go."

Then she thanked him for his time and took off, walking at a brisk pace, heading for the street.

Jeremy stood in the parking lot for the longest time, watching as she turned toward the bus stop.

Was she in some kind of trouble? Was she involved in an abusive relationship?

Had she—or the baby—been hurt?

Each time a question struck his mind, it exploded into several others. Maybe he should have tried harder to get her into the clinic.

Moments later, he glanced at his own watch. He had plenty of time on his hands and wasn't in any hurry. So, what the hell?

He strode back to the building he'd just left, entered the waiting room and made his way to the registration desk. Millie Arden was on duty today, so he asked if she had a minute.

"Of course, Doctor." The matronly woman with graying hair, a ruddy complexion and a warm smile looked up from her work. "What is it?"

"Do you remember seeing a mother in her twenties leave here a few minutes ago? She had light brown hair and was wearing jeans and a pink jacket. Her baby was wrapped in a blue shawl."

"Yes. She signed in as..." Millie glanced down at the list of patients in front of her and ran her finger along the names. "Here it is. Kirsten Allen."

Was that her actual name? Or a phony moniker for her to hide behind?

Again one question triggered several more.

"Has she visited the clinic before?" he asked.

"Just a moment. I'll check." Millie turned to her computer and, after a brief search, said, "It doesn't appear that she has."

Jeremy really ought to let it go, but he couldn't seem to do that. Not when Kirsten Allen had reminded him of the woman in his dream.

Hell, she even had a baby…

Surely it had been a coincidence, a fluke of some kind.

But during the short time that he'd spent with her, his blue funk had actually lifted—and it had yet to return.

After getting off the city bus at the intersection just a few blocks from Lone Star Lane, Kirsten carried little Anthony home, hoping to get back before her brother Max learned that she'd taken his son to the clinic.

Their relationship had always been a little shaky, more so right now. He resented what he called her interference in his life. Truth be told, she knew she'd clearly overstepped her bounds by taking Anthony for a medical evaluation, but she'd been desperate to find out if he was healthy, or if he had any undiagnosed problems that needed to be treated—a condition that could be serious.

Things like well-baby checkups and immunizations could wait until Max decided it was necessary, but her maternal instincts had kicked in and she felt compelled to make sure that Anthony's mother hadn't neglected something important.

And that was definitely possible. A couple days ago, Courtney, her brother's ex-girlfriend, had dropped off the precious little baby at Kirsten's house, announcing that Max was his father, that she'd grown tired of motherhood and that it was his turn to parent.

Kirsten had never liked Courtney, although she'd always kept her opinion to herself. But it had been difficult to hold her tongue when the flighty young woman handed the baby to a surprised Max, offering him only a car seat, a small package of disposable diapers and a bottle of formula. Then she'd taken off without even looking back.

It was safe to say that Anthony would probably be better off without Courtney in his life, especially since he was young enough not to be traumatized by her desertion. In fact, Kirsten couldn't understand how Max had gotten involved with a woman like her in the first place—or what he'd ever seen in her.

Still, she had to give her brother credit for stepping up to the plate. He might have been young and footloose in the past, but he had accepted responsibility for Anthony.

And, of course, so had Kirsten, which was why she'd taken him to the clinic today. But since the wait had been longer than she'd expected it to be, she would just have to be content to know that, from a physician's perspective, the baby boy appeared to be healthy.

Of course, a more thorough exam might reveal otherwise, so she still felt a twinge of uncertainty.

She knew that Max would see reason eventually and come to the conclusion that an appointment for a well-baby checkup was necessary. But that only made Kirsten think about immunizations, a subject Courtney had never even broached.

And that was another reason she'd insisted that Max try to find Courtney and quiz her about those kinds of details. Of course, her insistence had been her first misstep.

But old habits were hard to break. They were both adults now, and she really needed to remember not to push Max too hard, not to mother him.

He'd gotten tired of answering to his big sister about every little thing in his life, which she hoped was due to maturity rather than stubbornness. So he'd refused to look for Courtney, claiming that he could take care of the baby on his own.

Kirsten had her doubts, though. And that was why she'd snuck out to see a doctor while Max was job hunting. She knew he'd be upset if he learned that she'd taken on a parental role with the child and that he would accuse her of interfering and running his life again.

Of course that shouldn't surprise her. He'd been rebelling against her advice and instructions since he'd been a teenager. But this was different. Surely he would see that, wouldn't he?

When it came to the baby's health and welfare, he needed to put the past behind him and listen for a change.

As Kirsten reached the front door of her house, she dug in her purse for her keys, then she let herself inside.

"Are you ready for a bottle?" she asked Anthony, as she left the diaper bag in the entryway. The baby had been eating every three to four hours, so she figured he would be hungry soon.

Once in the living room, she put his blue shawl on the carpeted floor, then laid him down. "I'll be back in a minute, precious."

Anthony started to fuss, so she hurried to the kitchen and fixed him a bottle out of powdered formula and purified water.

She wished she had more experience with babies, that she'd done some babysitting as a teenager, but she was completely out of her league with that sort of thing.

The first couple days were hard, with her and Max learning through trial and error, but they were both finally catching on. In fact, she was really enjoying having a baby in the house. It made her wonder what it would be like to have a family of her own someday.

After carrying the bottle back to the living room, she picked up Anthony and settled into the overstuffed chair near the window. As she placed the nipple to his lips, he eagerly latched on, sucking and gulping as though he was starving.

Actually, now that she thought about it, he *did* have a hearty appetite, and that was definitely a sign of health. But that didn't mean she wouldn't try to sneak him back to the clinic again the next time Max would be gone for a couple hours. Hopefully, her car would be out of the shop by then, and she wouldn't have to ride the city bus, which had taken up way too much time.

Thank goodness she'd returned to the house before Max did.

At least she'd gotten a physician to at least take a quick look at the baby, even if it wasn't what you'd call a real exam.

She couldn't believe that she'd actually stopped a doctor in the parking lot today and asked him to look at

Anthony. She'd been so anxious—and thinking with her heart instead of her head, which she was prone to do.

But then the handsome physician with surfer-blond hair and soulful blue eyes had looked at her as if they'd met somewhere before, and she'd been knocked off balance. There was no way they'd ever crossed paths. She would have definitely remembered a gorgeous hunk like him.

Looking back, she wished she would have asked his name, but she hadn't been thinking straight.

In fact, he'd probably thought she was crazy, which was too bad. It would have been nice to have put her best foot forward when meeting the handsome orthopedic surgeon, a man who'd been exceptionally kind to her. After all, he hadn't needed to take time to talk to her, but he had. He'd even reached out and caressed Anthony's little cheek, right there in the parking lot.

Too bad she'd had a bus to catch so she would beat her brother home.

As Anthony guzzled down his bottle, Kirsten stopped him long enough to get a burp out of him—an effort he objected to with grunts and squawks.

When he finally let out a little belch, and she put the bottle back into his mouth, she heard the key sound in the lock.

Moments later, Max opened the door and stepped inside.

"So how was the job search?" she asked.

Her brother blew out a sigh. "No luck yet. So I guess you're stuck with us for a while."

That might be true about Max staying with her, but she certainly didn't feel stuck with Anthony.

"It's not a problem." Kirsten glanced at the sweet little baby who'd come to live with them. "I'm happy to help out while I can."

"But what happens when you get a call from another firm looking for an accountant? You've got a mortgage to pay, so you can't continue watching Anthony for me."

That was true. And Max would be hard-pressed to job hunt all day and watch over his son without help.

He didn't seem to be stressed about that, though. Or worried about the fact that he might not be able to afford day care *and* rent when he did manage to find employment.

"Well," Kirsten said, "I can watch him for the time being. We'll just have to take one day at a time."

And she shouldn't have any trouble doing that. She'd been taking one day at a time ever since she'd allowed Max to move in with her. But what else could she do? He was the only family she had left, and looking after him was a responsibility she'd always had.

Of course, she'd come to realize that some of her help over the years had bordered on enabling in many ways. The more money she gave him, the more he seemed to need.

Then, about two years ago, she'd read a book on tough love. It made sense that she wasn't really helping him by bailing him out all the time. So she'd told Max that she was finished taking care of him, that he was an adult and would have to fend for himself. He was twenty-four at the time and had just started dating Courtney, so he'd moved in with her for a while.

Lo and behold, he landed a good job at the feed store and kept it for nearly two years—until the owner sold the business.

Losing his job had been really tough on him—and it had been tough on Kirsten, too. But the layoff hadn't been his fault. His boss had decided to retire and sell the business, and since the new owner had a large family and planned to hire his kids to work for him, Max was let go.

Of course, that meant he could no longer pay his rent. So she'd offered to let him live with her until he found a new job.

She'd been afraid that they would both fall back into destructive old patterns, yet she didn't want Max to end up on the street when he'd been clearly trying hard to get his life on track. If she looked at the big picture, he deserved her help and a second chance.

And then Anthony had come along, immediately changing the dynamics of their brother-sister relationship and complicating things. After all, there was no way Kirsten would ask Max to leave or refuse to help him when that meant turning her back on Anthony, too.

She smiled at the child in her arms, his little eyes closed, his lips still tugging at the nipple.

"So how did things go for *you* today?" Max asked, as he plopped down on the sofa. "Did the baby give you any trouble?"

"We had a good day." She didn't dare tell him that

she'd taken Anthony to the clinic. She had to tread carefully with Max these days, not make him feel as though she was backing him into a corner. All she needed was for him to resent her interference, bolt and take little Anthony with him.

If he were to leave, where would he live? How would he support himself and a baby?

"How's your own job search coming?" he asked. "Did you get any nibbles from the résumés you filed with those online applications?"

"I'm still waiting to hear something." But she wouldn't actively seek a full-time position until Max found work and knew what his options were for day care.

"So you don't have any interviews scheduled?"

"No, but I'm really not worried yet." She had a healthy savings account, so she'd been able to pay the mortgage—so far.

"You know," Max said, "I've been thinking. The Red Rock Medical Center offers low-cost checkups. Maybe I ought to take Anthony one day next week."

Kirsten nearly jumped out of her chair, but she reeled in her excitement, knowing it was best to let Max think the whole idea had been his all along. Apparently, her hints had sunk in after she'd dropped the subject and let it go.

"You're probably right," she finally said in a ho-hum sort of way. "I could…" She caught herself, realizing that Max wanted to do the right thing, but for some reason, it was important for him to make those kinds of decisions on his own. "Well, I could look up the website on the computer and give you a phone number—in case you want to set up an appointment or ask questions."

He seemed to think on that for a while, then he said, "Sure, that would be okay."

She slowly released the breath she'd been holding.

Max wasn't a kid anymore. And he wasn't as irresponsible as he'd once been. She needed to remember that. She also needed to respect his decisions—whatever they were. And if that meant minding her sisterly *P*s and *Q*s, then so be it.

"Do you think Courtney would have taken Anthony for his shots?" she asked.

He'd refused to call Courtney, but maybe Kirsten could nudge him just a bit.

Max seemed to ponder that for a moment. "She used to hate going to the doctor herself, so something tells me she wouldn't have worried about taking Anthony."

Well, Courtney certainly hadn't appeared to have a very strong maternal instinct, but Kirsten bit her tongue, reminding herself to keep quiet and to let Max come to his own conclusions about his child's mother.

"I guess it's good that you're going to be the one raising him," Kirsten said. "He's going to need a daddy like you."

Max shrugged, although the hint of a smile suggested that her comment had pleased him. And she was glad that it had. Their relationship had taken a real turn for the better today, even if she was the one who'd learned a valuable lesson in dealing with Max, in trusting him to do the right thing.

"Do you want to go with me when I take Anthony to the clinic?" he asked.

The question both surprised and delighted her—but not because she needed to be involved in Anthony's care. She was happy to see that her relationship with her brother was finally on the mend.

"Sure," she said. "I can go with you as long as I don't have an interview scheduled."

"Thanks. I'd like you to be there. I'm not sure I want to see someone poke him with a needle."

Kirsten wasn't excited about seeing that, either.

"You know," Max said, "since things might change for you anytime on the job front, maybe I ought to schedule that appointment tomorrow. Would that be better for you?"

She bit down on her bottom lip, as though giving her schedule some real thought. "Yes, it would. I don't have anything planned for tomorrow."

"Good, then I'll call the clinic in the morning."

"All right. Just let me know what they tell you."

But she already knew. She'd called today, and they'd told her that her best chance of being seen today—when it wasn't an emergency—was to come in and wait her turn.

The thought of returning to the Red Rock Medical Center turned her heart on end, but not just because they would finally learn whether Anthony was as healthy as he appeared to be.

She was also hoping she'd run into a certain orthopedic surgeon.

Uh-oh. If she *did* see him again, and if he mentioned to Max anything about meeting her and Anthony in the parking lot…well, that might dash the strides they'd made in healing their relationship.

If so, she would just have to come clean with Max. And if he blew up about it? Then she'd face the consequences.

He might get angry and tell her to go home, which meant she'd miss out on spending further time with the handsome doctor. And that would be a shame.

Chapter Two

Even after a stop at the bookstore, Jeremy still arrived early at Red, one of the most popular restaurants in town.

Jose and Maria Mendoza, longtime friends of the Fortune family, had converted the old hacienda into a classy, romantic eatery with antique furnishings, woven tapestries and carefully selected pieces of Tejano art that nearly matched the original décor, much of which had been damaged two years ago in a fire which had turned out to be a case of arson. The Mendozas had been forced to close for a while. But with time and a great deal of effort, they'd restored the landmark.

As Jeremy entered, he was welcomed by Marcos Mendoza, who was temporarily managing Red for Jose and Maria. Some might think the handsome and personable young man had landed his position because of his relationship with the owners, but Jeremy knew that wasn't the case. Since taking over, Marcos had instigated some innovative and productive changes behind the scenes, and the restaurant seemed to be busier and more popular than ever.

"Welcome back to Red, Doc." Marcos reached out his arm in greeting. "How's it going?"

"Not bad." Jeremy shook the younger man's hand. "How about you?"

"Life is good. I can't complain." Marcos scanned the entry before returning his gaze to Jeremy. "Are you meeting someone?"

"My brother Drew and his wife."

"Then I'll take you back to the alcove. It'll give you a little more privacy. And when they arrive, I'll let them know where you are."

"Thanks." Jeremy usually preferred to eat in the courtyard, with the old-world style fountain that had been handcrafted with blue-and-white Mexican tile.

The Mendozas had heaters to make outdoor dining comfortable in the winter months, but it was already sprinkling, and the colorful umbrellas that provided shade from the sun weren't going to keep the rain off them.

As Marcos grabbed three menus, he asked, "When did the newlyweds get back from Vegas?"

The couple had eloped, and while it wasn't a secret, some of the details were sketchy. "They flew in last night."

"Oh, yeah? So they'll be staying in Red Rock?"

"I'm not sure what their plans are." Drew ran the San Diego office of Fortune Forecasting—although he'd been overseeing the entire operation in William's absence. And Deanna was his assistant. There was just so much that could be done via conference calls and email, so they'd both need to go back to work soon. But like Jeremy, Drew had been waiting on word about their father.

A beat of silence stretched between them, as they both considered the words Jeremy hadn't actually said.

"Still no word about your dad?" Marcos asked.

Jeremy slowly shook his head. "No, not yet."

"I'm sorry to hear that. Isabella came in earlier today to have lunch with some of her friends, but I didn't get a chance to ask her if there'd been any news."

Isabella, who'd married J. R. Fortune, Jeremy's oldest brother, was Marcos's sister. So Marcos was well aware of the details surrounding William's disappearance.

As they reached the empty table in the alcove, Marcos stopped and stepped to the side. "How's this?"

"Great."

Marcos removed one of the place settings, leaving three. "I'll have a server bring you some water and chips. Would you like to start off with a drink?"

"Sure. I'll have a Corona."

"You got it."

As Jeremy took a seat, he watched Marcos walk toward the bar. The ambitious young man had plans to open his own restaurant someday, and Jeremy had no doubt that he would do just that—and be successful.

Moments later, a young waitress with her long, dark hair pulled back in a ponytail brought the water, chips, salsa and his beer.

"Marcos said to tell you that the drink is on him," the woman said.

Jeremy thanked her, and as she went on her way, he got to his feet, stepped out of the alcove and scanned the area for Marcos.

He spotted him near the bar, where he was talking to the bartender and pointing out something on a shelf. When Jeremy caught the manager's eye, he lifted his longneck bottle and nodded in appreciation. Then he returned to his table and took a seat.

While waiting for Drew and Deanna, he reached for a warm tortilla chip and dipped it into the fresh salsa.

No one knew how to prepare Mexican food like the Mendozas, and Jeremy had made a point of stopping by Red at least once a week. Of course, each time he did, he often ran into one of the Fortunes or a Mendoza or two. The families had become good friends over the years. There also had been a few marriages along the way that bound them even closer—like that of J.R. and Isabella.

Jeremy had just reached for another chip when Drew and Deanna arrived. The two had been staying with J.R. and Isabella at Molly's Pride, where he assumed they would take up residence again until they needed to return to San Diego.

Drew's entire life had revolved around Fortune

Forecasting, the company William had started. But unlike his brothers, Jeremy had never wanted to take part in the family business. Instead, he'd gone to medical school. And up until the past year or so, he'd been perfectly content with that decision and the life he'd made for himself in Sacramento.

As Drew and Deanna reached the table, Jeremy stood and greeted the attractive redhead with a brotherly hug.

"You look especially pretty tonight," Jeremy told her.

And she did. Love and happiness radiated on her face, just as it did on Drew's.

"Thank you."

Drew pulled out a chair for her. As she took a seat, she flashed a loving smile at her new husband.

Jeremy couldn't help thinking that falling in love and getting married had made a big difference in his brother's entire demeanor, and as he made that decision, his thoughts naturally drifted to the mystery woman who'd stepped right out of his imagination and into his life just two hours earlier.

Drew reached for a chip. "We said six, didn't we?"

"Yes, but I finished early at the clinic." Jeremy motioned for their waitress, then returned his focus to his dinner companions. "So how was the wedding?"

"Absolutely beautiful." Deanna's eyes glimmered. "Your brother outdid himself with all the details, from the strawberries and champagne on the private flight to the long-stem red roses and the bridal bouquet waiting in the limousine to the beautiful little chapel where we were married at the stroke of midnight. It was very romantic."

A little surprised by it all, Jeremy studied his no-nonsense brother. "Who would have guessed that you had a romantic side?"

"You probably have one, too." His brother reached across the table and took Deanna's hand. "All you have to do is find the right woman."

Jeremy didn't know about that. He hadn't thought that he had a romantic bone in his body before, but he found his mind drifting in that direction ever since he ran into Kirsten Allen in the parking lot. Damn, that crazy dream must be making him soft.

As Drew and Deanna shared the details of the actual ceremony, Jeremy found himself drifting off, wondering if he'd prefer a big wedding or a small, intimate one. And that brought his thoughts back to the mystery woman.

He didn't believe in visions and premonitions, but for some wild reason, he couldn't quite shake the encounter he'd had with Kirsten or the feeling that he had to see her again.

"Are you listening?" Drew asked.

Jeremy glanced up, a little embarrassed that the couple had caught him gathering romantic wool, when he should have been listening. "I'm sorry. I've got a lot on my mind."

"Dad?" Drew asked.

"Him, too."

"Is it work-related? Is the medical group pressuring you to come back to Sacramento?"

"In a way, but…"

"Don't tell me." Drew leaned forward. "You've met a woman in Red Rock."

"No, not really." Jeremy glanced at his new sister-in-law, then back at the cocktail napkin he'd been shredding.

About that time, Deanna scooted her chair back and got to her feet. "If you guys will excuse me, I think I'll powder my nose."

Drew shot another loving look at his new wife, and something seemed to register between them, some form of silent, two-way communication.

Jeremy had seen his parents do that on occasion. Would he ever be able to communicate with a woman like that?

"What should I order for you?" Drew asked her. "A glass of wine?"

"That sounds good. Thanks."

As Deanna headed for the bathroom, Jeremy couldn't help thinking she'd made an excuse to leave so the brothers could talk in private, which was thoughtful but unnecessary. He really didn't want to talk to anyone about the wild direction his thoughts had been going.

After Deanna was out of hearing range, Drew said, "Okay, what's going on?"

Jeremy wasn't so sure he wanted to confide in his younger brother, but Drew wasn't a kid anymore. So he found himself revealing the dream he'd had and the woman he'd run into in the parking lot.

"Are you going to try to find her?" Drew asked.

Jeremy didn't know what to say, what to admit.

"Maybe you ought to give Ross a call. I'll bet he could make fast work of finding anyone."

Ross Fortune was their cousin and a private investigator, so the suggestion made sense. But Jeremy wouldn't go that far in trying to locate the mystery woman.

"I don't want to come off like some kind of stalker," he admitted. "Besides, Ross probably should focus his time on finding Dad, which he hasn't been able to do."

The truth of that statement echoed between them until Drew said, "I think we need to accept the fact that he's gone, Jeremy."

"You might be right, but I'm not able to do that yet."

"I know."

A pall fell over the brothers as they each tried to deal with their father's disappearance in their own way— Drew letting go and Jeremy refusing to give up.

When Deanna returned to the table, the conversation turned more upbeat, but Jeremy found himself sliding back into that blue funk that had been haunting him for months—even before he'd come to Red Rock for the wedding.

The only thing that seemed to help his mood was thinking about Kirsten Allen—if that was even her name.

Who was she?

What was her story?

And why in the world did it even seem to matter? Jeremy had never met a woman who could compete with his patients. He was a driven and dedicated physician, and as a result, he'd never married.

Maybe the dream and his interest in the mystery woman were just signs that his subconscious—and his hormones—were trying to rectify the situation.

Either way, something told him that he was going to have to find Kirsten Allen.

And if it took calling Ross and asking for help, then so be it.

The rain had moved on by morning, leaving a rainbow in the cloudy sky and puddles on the streets and sidewalks.

Over breakfast, Kirsten had admitted to Max that she'd taken the baby to the clinic yesterday. And she'd been right about his reaction; he'd bristled.

"I can't believe you'd do that without talking to me first," he'd said. "I don't want you to take over."

"I'm not trying to do that. I was just worried about his health, and...well, you're right. I shouldn't have gone over your head. I was wrong, and I'm sorry."

"When is it going to stop, Kirsten? You've been mothering me for years, and I've always resented it. Now you're trying to do it with Anthony. The way I see it, if you want a baby, maybe you should have one of your own."

She'd tensed at his harshness, but what he'd said was true. Even though she hadn't been around kids, she *had* always wanted to be a mom, to have a family. But that was *not* why she'd fought so hard to take good care of Max, to make sure he grew up happy and responsible.

It was not as though she wanted him to stay some kind of pseudo kid forever. Or that she'd needed someone to mother. "You're the only family I have left, Max. And I feel an obligation to make sure you're happy and able to support yourself."

"I'm doing fine on my own. I've just had a little setback with the job and all." He raked a hand through his hair. "You're my big sister, and I get that. But I'm sick of you constantly trying to tell me what to do, how to feel, what to say. It's my life. And I want to make my own way—right or wrong."

Before she could respond, he added, "I've been on my own for two years—paying my rent, being a man. And you have no idea how it grates on me to have to live with my sister again, to accept your handouts. Believe me, all I want to do is land a new job and get out of here."

In her heart of hearts, she knew that when Max moved out, it would be the best for her, too. She needed to let go of him and focus on creating a place for herself in Red Rock.

"I'm sorry," she'd said, repeating the apology she'd made earlier. "I only meant to be helpful. And you're right. Anthony is your son, your responsibility. I'll do my best to back off."

The fight had seemed to fizzle out of him at her acquiescence, so she'd gone on to say, "I'm trying, Max. *Really,* I am. You're not a kid anymore. And I need to trust you to make the right decisions for yourself and now for your son. But you'll have to be a little patient with me. Old habits are hard to break."

"I still can't believe that you took him to the clinic without my permission. What did you tell them? That you were his mother?"

"I wouldn't have lied. But truthfully, I hadn't really thought that far."

He'd scoffed, and she realized just how impulsive she'd been.

"I can make a hundred excuses for what I did," she'd admitted, "but I'm not going to do that. You're Anthony's father. And you're right. I overstepped my bounds. From now on, I'm going to step back and let you live your own life—right, wrong or indifferent. Those decisions are yours to make—not mine."

Max kept quiet all through breakfast, and about the time she'd decided that he wasn't going to let her go to the clinic with him, he relented.

"Okay, Kirsten. I need you more than I'm comfortable admitting. Maybe that's why I'm fighting you so hard." He blew out a sigh. "I'd really like you to go with me—as a second pair of ears—but *not* as my spokesperson."

A part of her wanted to back off completely and let him handle it *all* on his own, but after Courtney had arrived with the baby a couple days ago and announced that Max was the father, they'd both been caught off guard. And together they'd scrambled to buy diapers, formula, bottles and a little bed for him to sleep in.

It had been almost overwhelming, yet at the same

time, there had been moments where she and Max had actually been a team for the first time in ages. And that had given her hope that the troubles they'd had in the past would soon be behind them. That they were on their way to becoming the family they'd been before their father had abandoned them, before their mother had died.

Through trial and error, frustration and smiles, she and Max had been learning how to take care of Anthony.

So the baby's arrival had turned out to be a good thing, forcing the two of them to work together for a change.

"All right," Kirsten had agreed. "You've got yourself a deal."

An hour later, they found themselves back at the clinic, checking in with a matronly receptionist whose badge announced that her name was Millie.

"Just take a seat," Millie said. "It shouldn't be too long. You arrived here early today, which is good. We always get backed up in the late afternoon."

Max shot Kirsten a glance, but she bit her tongue. She'd apologized for bringing Anthony yesterday, but she certainly wasn't going to grovel. What was done was done.

When they took seats in the waiting room, Max held the baby, so Kirsten picked up a magazine and thumbed through it. She feared that she was enabling Max again by being here, by babysitting Anthony and by offering them both a place to stay. But she couldn't very well throw out him and the baby.

She'd meant what she'd said about boundaries, though.

So how did she go about encouraging Max to find a job and to help out around the house, when he'd probably see that encouragement as interference?

She stole a glance at her brother, who held little Anthony with stiff arms and a tender expression. Anyone looking at him could tell he had feelings for the baby, even though he'd only known about him for a short time. It was obvious that he wanted to do right by his son. That, she decided, counted for a great deal.

As the door swung open, and a nurse called an elderly woman for her appointment, Kirsten found herself scanning the back room of the clinic, trying to spot the handsome orthopedic surgeon she'd met yesterday.

But what if she *did* see him? What then?

A man like that was probably only interested in sophisticated, stylish women with high-profile careers and social connections.

Still, each time the door to the exam rooms opened, each time someone in a lab coat walked by, Kirsten couldn't help searching for the doctor with sun-streaked hair and intensive blue eyes who had consumed her thoughts.

Jeremy was looking over an X-ray of a fractured scaphoid bone in a teenage boy's hand, a break that had actually occurred years earlier.

Last night, the kid had fallen during a basketball game and twisted his wrist. And since he was still complaining of pain this morning, his mother had brought him into the clinic, suspecting that he might have a serious sprain or a break. But the fall had only aggravated an old injury. And it was a good thing that it had brought him in today. If the original break had continued to go untreated, the teenager might have eventually lost the full use of his hand.

As it was, he would need surgery and a bone graft to correct it.

"Dr. Fortune?"

Jeremy turned to see Millie, the receptionist, standing in the doorway.

"I'm sorry to bother you, Doctor, but Kirsten Allen is here again. You know, the woman you were asking me about yesterday?"

Jeremy's pulse rate spiked at the news, but he maintained an unaffected facial expression. "Thanks, Millie. Where is she?"

"In the waiting room."

As much as Jeremy would like to go out and talk to her, he had to discuss his findings with the teenage patient and his mother who were waiting for the results of the X-ray.

"Do me a favor," Jeremy said. "Can you have Kirsten called into an exam room? And then let me know where I can find her?"

Millie's brow twitched, as if she found the request a little unusual, but she didn't ask his reason for it. Instead, she nodded. "I'll see what I can do."

"Thank you. I appreciate that." Jeremy didn't usually ask for favors, like moving people up in line. But Kirsten had left yesterday without waiting to be seen, and he didn't want that to happen again. Not before he had a chance to see her and talk to her again.

While Millie went to do as she was asked, Jeremy returned to the exam room to tell the teenager and his mother about the fracture and explain the surgery and healing process.

Ten minutes later, he made his way to room four, which had been assigned to Anthony Allen, Kirsten's infant son.

He knocked lightly, then opened the door, eager to see the attractive woman again, to get a chance to talk to her. But when he spotted a man in the room with her, his heart slammed against his chest.

Damn. She was married—or at least involved with someone.

Well, of course she was. What made him even think that she might not be?

A striking resemblance to the dream woman, that was what. And an overactive imagination for another. See what happened when a man read too much into a random dream and followed a hunch?

Trying not to stammer or to reveal his surprise, Jeremy reached out his hand to introduce himself to the baby's father. "Hello, I'm Dr. Fortune."

"Max Allen. Are you here to examine Anthony?"

"No, I…" Jeremy glanced at Kirsten, wondering if she had any idea why he was actually here.

Hell, how could she? He was still struggling to make sense of the thoughtless blunder himself.

He returned his focus on her husband and tried to

make light of it all. "Actually, I met Mrs. Allen in the parking lot yesterday. She'd spent a lot of time in the waiting room and hadn't been seen, so I wanted to make sure she got in quickly today."

Max stiffened. "Yeah, well, she shouldn't have done that."

Done *what?* Left without seeing a pediatrician? Talked to a man in the parking lot?

"Excuse me?" Jeremy pressed, picking up some negative vibes and hoping he hadn't gotten her in trouble.

"Kirsten brought Anthony here yesterday without my permission." Max tossed a frown her way.

Now it was Jeremy's turn to tense and give out some negative vibes. What kind of man controlled his wife like that?

"Maybe I'd better explain," Kirsten said. "First of all, I'm Max's sister. And I was babysitting his son yesterday." She turned to the young man beside her. "I shouldn't have taken it upon myself to bring the baby for a checkup without getting Max's okay."

Jeremy was still struggling to understand what Max's problem was, but that didn't stop him from realizing that Kirsten wasn't married to Max and being relieved at the news.

Just then, the door opened, and Jim Kragen, a pediatrician, stepped into the now crowded room. "Sorry. I was told to come to exam room four."

"You're in the right place," Jeremy told his colleague. "I just stopped in here for a minute. I'll leave you to your patient."

As Dr. Kragen stepped inside, Jeremy made his way to the door.

"Excuse me a minute," Kirsten said to her brother and to the pediatrician. "I'll be right back."

Was she following Jeremy out?

Apparently so. And he couldn't help feeling a rush of pleasure. That was, until he glanced at Max, who seemed to be annoyed at her departure.

If Jeremy didn't know better, he'd think that Max was sizing him up and finding him lacking. But maybe that was only his imagination.

When Kirsten and Jeremy left the small room and shut the door behind them, she said, "Thank you for coming to check on us."

"No problem. I knew you were worried about the baby, so I wanted to make sure you finally got to see a doctor."

"Actually, I kind of panicked yesterday, thinking Max wouldn't get around to making an appointment for the baby himself. But Anthony is really sweet, and he's eating well. So Dr. Kragen will probably say he's doing fine." She tucked a strand of hair behind her ear, revealing a small diamond stud. "You probably think I'm a worrywart, but I've never really been around small children before. And up until a few days ago, Max didn't even know he was a father. His ex-girlfriend just dumped the baby on him—well, on us, actually. Max is living with me for the time being. So we've had a crash course on child care and still have a lot to learn."

"How long will your brother have Anthony?"

"Permanently, I guess." Kirsten blew out a soft sigh. "And I'm sure that's for the best. His girlfriend isn't very maternal."

Was Kirsten maternal? Was she the kind of woman who'd make a good partner for a man like him?

It was hard to say without knowing more about her.

"If I'd done more babysitting as a teenager," she added, "I might not feel so out of my league. But I'm…well… my brother and I are both novices."

"I'm sure you're doing fine."

"Thanks for the vote of confidence." She flashed him a pretty smile. "You should have seen us shopping that first day. We had to buy just about everything other than a car seat, and we didn't have a clue what we were going to need. It must have been comical to anyone watching us."

"You're a good sister," he said.

Her smile faded some. "I try to be."

Something told him that Max didn't always make it easy for her, but that was only a hunch. And Jeremy rarely went with his gut feelings, even though that was exactly what he'd done when he had first spotted Kirsten in the parking lot.

They stood like that for a moment, studying each other in the narrow hallway.

She gave a little nod toward the closed door of the exam room. "I guess I'd better get back in there and make sure I don't miss anything important."

Jeremy didn't want to let her go without having some way of getting in touch with her, so he reached into the pocket of his lab coat and pulled out one of his cards. Then he took the pen he kept handy, jotted his cell number on the back and handed it to her. "If you need anything, give me a call. Like I told you before, I'm not a pediatrician, but I'll try to answer any questions you or your brother might have."

She took the card, then blessed him with a smile. The light in her eyes and a single dimple in her cheeks just about turned his stubborn heart on edge. "Thank you, Dr. Fortune. I really appreciate this. I'll try not to bother you, though."

"You won't. And call me Jeremy."

Her hand lifted to the silver necklace she wore, and she fingered the delicate heart charm that lay against the soft cotton fabric of her light blue T-shirt. Her head cocked slightly to the side, as if she was considering whatever might be brewing between them.

Of course, there wasn't anything going on between them. At least, not yet.

"So you're not married?" he asked.

"No, I'm not."

A grin tugged at his own lips. He realized that now wasn't the time to ask her out, but he wondered if her thoughts were drifting in that direction, too.

The attraction seemed to be mutual, although his interest in her had been heightened by that crazy dream he'd had. And while his rational nature knew there hadn't been anything prophetic about it, he didn't want to let her slip away again without at least having a deeper conversation with her.

If he had her number, he'd give her a follow-up phone call tomorrow. Then he might even ask her to dinner. But he didn't have her number and wouldn't go as far as to ask for it.

If there'd been anything to his dream, if his attraction to her was due to something bigger than either of them, then she would have to call him.

And he'd just have to wait and see if she did.

Chapter Three

While Max ran into the pharmacy to pick up some vitamins and a special diaper rash ointment Dr. Kragen had recommended, Kirsten waited in the car with the sleeping baby secured in his seat in the back.

She'd been relieved to hear that Anthony was healthy and thriving. And now that her worries had been some-what stilled, she couldn't help thinking about the kindness of Dr. Fortune—or rather, Jeremy. He seemed to have taken a special interest in her, although she couldn't say how or why she'd come to that conclusion.

It was in the way he looked at her, she supposed. The way their gazes seemed to connect and the hormones and pheromones that seemed to spark whenever he was near.

She reached into her purse and pulled out his business

card. She'd been a little surprised that he'd given it to her—and pleased that he had.

But how many doctors actually gave out their personal phone numbers? Not many, she suspected.

She turned the card over and looked on the back, where the numbers were written in bold strokes—clear and legible, unlike the proverbial doctor's scrawl she would have expected to see.

He'd given her permission to call him, but would she? *Should* she?

Maybe she could use the results of their visit with Dr. Kragen as an excuse to call him now. At least, he would then have a record of her number.

She hesitated only a moment before taking her cell phone from her purse and dialing the number he'd given her.

Jeremy answered on the third ring. "Hello?"

Her words jammed in her throat as she contemplated hanging up before indentifying herself. But she felt compelled to finish what she'd started. "Dr. Fortune? This is Kirsten Allen. I just wanted to let you know that Dr. Kragen told us Anthony looks good and appears to be healthy."

"I'm glad to hear that."

"I'd worried about not having any of Anthony's medical records, but Dr. Kragen ordered a blood test to check to see if he's had any of his immunizations yet. So that's one less thing for me to stress about."

"Jim's one of the top pediatricians in the county, so

you were in good hands. He has a private practice, but he works one day a month at the clinic."

Kirsten bit down on her lip as she contemplated a response. She wasn't ready to end the call, although they really had nothing else to talk about.

"Well," she said, "I just wanted to thank you again for being so nice to me…to us."

"It was my pleasure, Kirsten."

As silence stretched across the line, she suddenly wondered if she'd been wrong to think that he was interested in her in any way other than that of a kindhearted professional.

"Well…"

"Would you like to have dinner some night?" he asked, throwing her a curve.

Her heart dropped like dead weight, then rumbled back to life. "That sounds like fun."

Fun? She rolled her eyes. Why hadn't she given him a more sophisticated answer, one more grown-up and better suited to a doctor's dinner date?

"How about tomorrow night?" he asked.

So soon?

Goodness. Where would they go? What would she wear? Yet in spite of the questions and the fly-by-night insecurities that pelted her, she found herself saying, "Sure."

"I'm looking forward to it," he said.

So was she, even if a swarm of butterflies had settled in her stomach.

After he asked for her address and she gave it to him, he said, "I'll see you tomorrow night."

When the call ended, she sat dumbfounded for a while, the cell phone still in her hand.

Had she just imagined that conversation? Had the handsome doctor just asked her out to dinner? Would she have the right clothes to wear? Would she say the correct things?

Of course she would. She was a college graduate, for Pete's sake—an accountant. Okay, so she was unemployed at the moment. But that was only temporary. She had the skills and the résumé to land another job soon.

A knock sounded at the passenger window, and she turned to see Max waiting to get into the car. So she hit the unlock button and slid the cell phone back into her purse.

"Who were you talking to?" he asked, as he climbed in.

"Dr. Fortune. He asked me out to dinner tomorrow night, and I told him yes. Do you think you'll be okay by yourself with Anthony?"

Max chuffed. "I don't believe this."

"Believe what?"

"You brought Anthony to the clinic yesterday so you could hook up with a doctor? How long has that been going on?"

"What are you talking about?"

"Your crush on Dr. Fortune."

"You're imagining things. I don't have a crush on him."

"Then what's going on?"

She had no idea. She found Jeremy Fortune attractive and the thought of dating him exciting. And for some wild reason, he seemed to find her attractive, too.

"It's no big deal," she told her brother. "Like I said, I met him in the parking lot yesterday. We've talked briefly a couple of times, and he asked me out."

"A doctor seems to be a cut above your usual boy-friend. Don't you think a guy like that is out of your league?"

Jeremy Fortune *might* be, but that didn't keep Kirsten from smiling—or from dreaming about being with him.

It was all very Cinderella-ish, she supposed. And even if she didn't have stepsisters to tell her that she wasn't princess material, she didn't need them to. Between her own doubts and Max's, she was already having second thoughts about her date with the handsome doctor.

But she shook off a few lingering insecurities, as well as any possible shortcomings she might have, and looked forward to tomorrow night.

Jeremy pulled up along the curb of an older, two-story home in a quiet Red Rock neighborhood. It wasn't anything like the yard or porch he'd seen in his dream, but then why would it be?

The house in his dream had only been a random nocturnal image, he reminded himself. It didn't mean anything.

Sure, when he'd spotted Kirsten in the parking lot of

the clinic, he'd thought she bore a slight resemblance to the woman he'd envisioned, but that was just a coincidence. He would have found her attractive anyway. The similarity had only opened his eyes and allowed him to escape his troubles for the time being.

After parking his car, he made his way to the front door and rang the bell.

Max answered, a scowl plastered to his face. He invited Jeremy in, but he didn't crack a smile.

"How's it going?" Jeremy asked.

"Okay." Max closed the door. "My sister will be out in a minute. Have a seat."

Jeremy scanned the tidy room, noting the simple furnishings that had been carefully placed around the room: a beige sofa adorned with brightly colored decorator pillows, a wrought-iron floor lamp with a matching shade, dark wood furniture.

Red candles and a few photographs were displayed on the mantel over a brick fireplace.

The living room had a cozy, welcoming feel about it, and he could tell Kirsten took pride in her home.

Max sat in a recliner, his eyes glued to the television, watching a college basketball game. A portable travel crib rested beside him, where Anthony lay on his back, kicking his feet and watching a dinosaur mobile.

"Who's playing?" Jeremy asked, taking one last stab at being friendly.

Max was so focused on the game that it took him a moment to respond. "Oklahoma State at Texas A&M."

"What's the score?"

"The Aggies are up by five."

Silence again.

Jeremy decided to let it go. He was just about to take a seat when Kirsten entered the living room wearing a simple black dress and heels. Her hair had been swept up into a twist, revealing that small pair of diamond studs.

She wore only the slightest bit of makeup: mascara to highlight those pretty blue eyes, a pink shade of lipstick to accentuate a natural pout.

He'd known she was attractive in denim and T-shirts. But the transformation from casual tomboy to classy dinner date was jaw-dropping.

"You look great," he said.

Her cheeks flushed when she smiled. "Thank you."

Max lifted the remote toward the television and turned down the volume. Then he stood, crossed his arms and shifted his weight to one hip. "So where are you guys going?"

Jeremy hadn't suffered through a date-night interrogation since he'd been a teenager going to his last high school prom. And it prickled him to have to go through it now, especially from a man who was probably more than ten years his junior. But he shook off his irritation and played the game. "I thought we'd go to Bernardo's, the new Italian restaurant that just opened up a few blocks down the street from Red. That is, if Kirsten doesn't mind."

"Bernardo's sounds good to me." She offered him a breezy smile, then grabbed her purse from a small table near the door. "I'll see you later, Max. You can call me if you have a problem with Anthony."

"I'll be okay."

Good, because Jeremy was looking forward to putting some distance between them. What was that guy's problem?

Jeremy opened the door, then followed Kirsten out of the house. Moments later, they were in his rental car and headed into town for dinner.

"I'm afraid I need to apologize for my brother's rudeness," Kirsten said. "His life has been turned upside down, so he's been a little testy with everyone lately."

"No apology necessary."

"I know. But…" She pursed her lips. "I guess everyone has their cross to bear. And Max is mine."

Jeremy wasn't sure why she felt that way. "How old is he? Twenty-four?"

"Actually, he's twenty-six."

"Then I'd say it's probably time for him to move on and make a life of his own."

"I wish it were that easy." Kirsten glanced out her window at the passing scenery, then back to Jeremy. "He's between jobs, so I can't very well boot him out into the street. And now that he has Anthony…"

"I can see how that would complicate things." Jeremy had a strong sense of family loyalty, too, so he understood why she was supportive of Max. "How's it working out?"

"It's been tough." She gave a half shrug. "But there's

not much I can do about it until he lands another job and can move out."

"What kind of position is he looking for?"

"Anything at this point. I think he wants to move as badly as I'd like to see him go. But he doesn't have a high school diploma, which limits his options when it comes to finding something that will pay the rent, and now he has day-care expenses to cover."

"That's too bad."

"I know." She took a deep breath, then sighed softly. "I tried to talk him into getting his GED and picking up some college courses, but he refused to even consider it."

"Why?"

"I'm afraid it was probably because I suggested it." She rested her hands on top of the small black purse that sat in her lap. "And because he's never been particularly ambitious. After he dropped out of high school, he just drifted from job to job for one reason or another."

"In that case, you might not be doing him any favors by letting him stay with you."

"Actually, two years ago he was hired on at the feed store and was able to keep that one until a couple weeks ago. He really seemed to like it, but when the new management took over, they laid everyone off, and Max was back at square one."

Jeremy was glad to see that her brother had managed to hold a job, but he couldn't understand why the guy wouldn't try to take the GED exam or improve his chances of getting a better paying position.

He knew he should keep his thoughts to himself, but he said, "Maybe, if he won't take your advice, it might be time for you to back off and let him captain his own ship, even if it has leaks."

"I'm sure you're right. But my biggest fault is that I tend to think with my heart more than my head."

Learning that bit of news about Kirsten probably ought to throw up a red flag for a guy who'd always been methodical and rational, but Jeremy found it appealing that she had a soft heart. Maybe because she reminded him of his mother in that way.

Molly Fortune had been the one to encourage Jeremy to follow his dream and go to medical school. Not that anyone had given him a hard time when he chose not to work at Fortune Forecasting. His dad and brothers had been pretty supportive, too. But it had been Molly's proud smile at his graduation that had made it all worthwhile.

He shot a glance across the seat at Kirsten, wondering if she had any other qualities that would remind him of his mother.

Molly had been a dynamic woman—warm, loving and a real mama bear when it came to her husband and her five sons. So when she passed away four years ago, the entire family had taken it hard. But Jeremy had a feeling he might have grieved for her even more than the others had.

He hadn't spent that much time with her after he moved to Sacramento and started his practice with a prominent orthopedic medical group, but he'd valued her opinion and her unwavering support, even if he didn't always take her advice. And she'd always been just a phone call away.

Of course, he'd accepted her loss and moved on with his life, but her death had left a hole.

He looked across the seat at Kirsten and couldn't help wondering if a loving wife and a family of his own would make him feel whole again. He hoped so—whether that woman turned out to be Kirsten or not.

As he pulled into the parking lot at Bernardo's, he stole another glance at his lovely dinner date.

They'd only met a couple days ago, so he had no way of knowing whether she was the kind of woman he was looking for or not.

But he had every intention of finding out.

Kirsten sat across a romantic, candlelit table from Jeremy, listening to him tell her about his day at the clinic. It was clear that he enjoyed his work and cared about his patients, and she found herself smiling at just about everything he said.

But she wasn't the only one who was enjoying the evening so far. Jeremy's body language and ready smile told her that their date had gotten off to a good start.

"What do you do for a living?" he asked.

"I'm an accountant." She lifted her water goblet and took a sip.

"Where do you work?"

She'd hoped that wouldn't come up, but realized it might. "I'm between jobs at the moment, but I'll get another position quickly. I've got some great letters of recommendation and a solid résumé. It's just a matter of time."

He smiled, then took a bite of his manicotti.

She didn't want him to give too much thought about the only similarity she and Max had other than their family resemblance, so she decided to shift the focus of the conversation back to him. "The clinic is lucky to have you. Do you ever think you'll work in private practice?"

"Actually, I do have a practice—in Sacramento. I'm just volunteering my time at the clinic."

Her heart cramped at the thought of him leaving town, which seemed to be what he was saying. "What brought you to Red Rock? And how long will you be here?"

"I came for my father's wedding, which was supposed to have taken place last month. And I'll be in town as long as it takes to…" Jeremy glanced down at his plate, then back at Kirsten.

The sun-bleached streaks in his hair glistened in the candlelight, and his eyes locked on hers. She sensed the emotion in his voice before he even spoke a word.

"My dad disappeared on what should have been his wedding day, and he hasn't been seen or heard from since. There was no way I could leave town, so I took a leave of absence. That allows me to stay in Red Rock until he's found."

Her heart broke for him as he continued to give her the details about the vehicle accident, about the police investigation that went nowhere. "I don't usually rely on hunches and feelings, but I... Well, I believe he's going to turn up."

She reached across the table, placed her hand over his and felt his warmth, his strength in spite of his vulnerability. She understood the feeling all too well. Her own father had run off when she was fourteen. And she'd hung on to the belief that he would return, that he'd never abandon her and the family.

But he hadn't come back. And she'd had to face the hurt, the disappointment.

Jeremy's eyes locked onto Kirsten's, revealing that he might not be as hopeful as he'd said he was, as if he'd needed her agreement and support. It was the kind of emotional reaction she'd always hoped to get from her brother—the sense of unity and understanding, the realization that she was connecting with someone she cared about. Yet it was all that and more.

Something else simmered in his gaze, something warmed by the glow of the candlelight, by the romantic music playing softly in the background and by the hum of pheromones that permeated every breath they took.

Jeremy Fortune was a man to take seriously. And with time, he might even prove to be a man that she could promise to love, honor and cherish—given the chance to get to know him better. But time was a luxury they didn't have. He was only in Red Rock temporarily and would be going back to California soon.

So she slowly drew her hand away, her fingertips skimming over the top of his knuckles as she did so.

She shouldn't get any romantic ideas. This might be

the date of a lifetime for her, but it was just a diversion for him. He wasn't in any position to form a relationship right now, so she'd be foolish to let her thoughts drift in that direction. After all, he'd be leaving town eventually.

And where would that leave her?

Jeremy's skin continued to tingle where Kirsten had touched him—and so did his heart. Her compassion, her understanding, did something to him. But before he could ponder just what that might be, the waiter who'd introduced himself as Gordon when they'd first been seated, asked, "Are you ready for me to take your plates?"

"Yes, I'm finished," Kirsten said. "Thank you."

Jeremy let the waiter pick up his dinner plate, too.

"Can I interest you in our dessert menu?" the young man asked.

Jeremy wasn't ready for the evening to end, so he said, "Sure. Let's see what you have."

The waiter had no more than walked away when Jeremy's cell phone vibrated.

Ever since his father's disappearance, he made sure the phone was always handy. There was no telling when a call might come in, saying his dad had been found. So he checked the display and, after noting the Sacramento area code, recognized a familiar number.

"Excuse me a moment," he told Kirsten. "This is a colleague from Sacramento."

"No problem. I understand."

When Jeremy answered, Jack Danfield said, "How's it going? Any word on your father?"

"No, not yet. I'm in the middle of dinner. Can I give you a call back later?"

"Yes, but first let me tell you the reason for my call. I have a twelve-year-old boy in the E.R. who was involved in a car accident. He has multiple fractures in both legs. He's had some arterial damage, and I'm afraid we might need to amputate. But I wanted to talk to you first. You had that case last summer that was similar, and you were able to save the limb."

Jeremy looked at his watch. He needed more details, and the consult would not only take time, but it was also going to require all of his concentration. "I'll give you a call in about ten minutes, Jack. Will that be okay?"

"Certainly."

When the line disconnected, Jeremy glanced across the table at his dinner companion, who seemed to be growing prettier by the minute. "I'm really sorry, Kirsten. I've got a long-distance consultation that just might help save a boy's leg, and it's important that I spend some time on it. I'm afraid I'm going to have to end our dinner early."

She reached for the strap of her purse that hung on the back of her chair. "There's no need to explain, Jeremy. I understand."

He motioned for the waiter, who returned to the table with the menus in hand.

"I'm sorry," Jeremy told him. "We're going to have

to pass on dessert. And I'll need the bill as soon as you can bring it."

"Yes, sir. I'll be right back."

Five minutes later, Jeremy and Kirsten were in his car and on the road.

"I'm really sorry to end our evening like this," he said.

"Don't be. I understand. Your patients come first. I just hope everything turns out okay for that poor boy."

So did Jeremy.

He pulled along the curb in front of her house and parked. After getting out of the car, they walked to her front door. He really needed to return Jack's call as quickly as possible, but he couldn't help lingering on the porch just a moment longer.

Did he dare kiss Kirsten good-night?

How deeply did he want to get involved with her?

At this point, he could pretty much cut bait and run. But he'd enjoyed their time together so far, and there was so much more he wanted to know about her.

"Thank you for dinner," she said. "Bernardo's was a great choice."

"You're welcome. But I still owe you a dessert."

"No, you don't." She looked up at him and smiled, her blue eyes glimmering in the porch light. "The food was so good, I didn't leave room for anything more."

They stood like that for a moment—gazing at each other, hanging on to the moment. If Jeremy had all the time in the world, would she invite him inside?

Again, the question of a good-night kiss returned full force. Should he or shouldn't he?

He wasn't sure why he bothered to even ponder the question. The urge to kiss her was almost overwhelming.

Oh, what the hell. He placed a hand on her cheek, felt the silk of her skin, the curve of her jaw.

As her head tilted up slightly and her lips parted, it was all the encouragement he needed.

Chapter Four

Kirsten didn't know what she'd expected to happen when Jeremy walked her to the front door, but certainly not *this*, not a soul-stirring good-night kiss.

Of course, she'd seen it coming when his gaze reached deep inside her, when he touched her cheek with a lover's caress. And she'd been filled with anticipation as their lips met.

The moment was so heart-stopping, so magical, that she was afraid to breathe for fear it was all a dream and she'd wake up alone in her bed, her arms wrapped around her pillow.

And while it was really happening, she was spell-bound by his heady, woodland scent, by the warmth of his breath and the heat of his touch.

As the kiss deepened and their lips parted, his tongue

brushed hers, making her knees go weak. So she reached for his waist to steady herself. As she did so, he slipped his arms around her, drawing her close, kissing her until she was tempted to drag him inside and see what happened next.

Oh, lordy. If this was the way Jeremy kissed a woman good-night, she wondered what it would be like to welcome him into her bed, into her…life.

She'd have to get control of her runaway thoughts and emotions, though. She couldn't allow herself to get swept away in a romantic fantasy with the handsome doctor, no matter how enjoyable their evening together had been, no matter how arousing his good-night kiss was.

It was crazy to think this was anything more than it was—a pleasant dinner that had come to a nice end. One day in the not-so-distant future, he was going to return to his medical practice in California, and she'd probably end up being a fleeting memory on his part. But there was a chance that he would mean a lot more than that to her. So for that reason alone, she needed to end this sweet assault before she lost her head completely.

Yet her body found it hard to comply with common sense, leaving it all up to him.

As Jeremy broke the kiss and released her from his embrace, she tried to shake off the effects of the lingering magic to no avail. Her pulse was racing and her mind was scrambling to imagine something romantic developing between them.

Still, she knew better than to waste her time thinking about those kinds of possibilities. Not when there were twice as many reasons a relationship between her and Jeremy would never work out.

But as he looked deep into her eyes, she couldn't seem to wrap her mind around a single one of them.

"Thanks for a nice evening," he said softly. "I'll give you a call tomorrow."

Still stunned by the sweet but arousing kiss, she was afraid to speak for fear she'd stumble over the words, so she merely nodded.

When he turned and strode toward his car, she continued to watch him. She really ought to go inside the house, but her legs didn't seem to be working any better than her voice.

Once he reached the street and stood beside the driver's door, he paused long enough to look over the top of the sedan and smiled. "Good night, Kirsten."

She lifted her hand to wave, realizing that her fingers had been resting against her lips, which still tingled from the kiss they'd shared.

"Good night," she managed to say.

As he climbed into his car, she realized just how appropriate her parting words had been.

It had been a *good* night indeed.

After dropping off Kirsten at her house, Jeremy pulled into the nearest shopping center and parked under a fluorescent light, not wanting to wait any longer before returning Jack Danfield's call.

Even though he was still reeling over the heated kiss he'd shared with Kirsten, he had to shake the giddiness and focus. As he did so, he dialed his colleague's number.

Jack had been waiting with the results of the X-ray and CT scan, so they discussed the details of the surgery as well as all the complications that could arise. Thanks to the efforts of modern technology, Jeremy had been able to see the scans and pictures on his iPhone, although he would have felt better about his counsel if he'd been standing next to Jack, viewing the images together.

Nearly an hour later, Jeremy drove back to the Double Crown Ranch and parked near the barn, which had been rebuilt after an arsonist had set it on fire a couple years back.

There were still lights on in the expansive, eight-bedroom house, a solid adobe structure, with sand-colored walls and rough-hewn wooden beams, which meant Lily was still awake.

Good. That would give him a chance to talk to her and ask about her day. They'd both come to depend upon each other after William's disappearance.

Using the key ring remote, Jeremy locked the car, then strode along the curved adobe walkway to the steps that led up to the large, antique wooden door.

Each time Jeremy passed through the arched entryway and opened the wrought-iron gate to the inner courtyard, with its abundant garden of native perennials and flowering vines, he felt as though he'd come home.

He had a lot of memories of the ranch where he'd spent most of his summer vacations as a kid, and whenever he stepped on the property, all those sunny days of hard work and cowboy fun came back to him.

Aunt Lily and Uncle Ryan had been good to him, as well as his brothers. So he was determined to "be there" for Lily now, while she was awaiting word from or about his dad.

After letting himself into the tiled foyer, he called out, "Lily? I'm home."

The woman—who should have been his stepmother by now—said, "I'm in the great room, Jeremy."

He followed her voice, finding her seated in one of the custom-made leather chairs, a tea service set out in front of her on a glass-topped table.

She brightened when he entered the room. "How was your day?"

"It was great." Not only had he enjoyed having dinner with Kirsten, but he'd been part of the medical effort to save a young boy's leg. "How about yours?"

"It was all right."

Actually, Jeremy realized, nothing would ever be "all right" again until William Fortune returned to his family—one way or another.

"Would you like something to drink?" Lily asked. "I can pour you a cup of tea, but there are decanters of bourbon and Scotch in the bar, if you'd like something stronger."

"Thanks, but I'll just get myself some water. I'll be back in a minute."

When Jeremy returned with his glass, he took a seat on one of the chairs facing his aunt.

At sixty-five, Lily was still an attractive woman. Her Apache and Spanish heritage provided her with high cheekbones and large dark eyes, lending her an exotic beauty.

"I don't like to think of you staying home all alone," Jeremy said, although he knew why she did. She wanted to be near the phone in the event that William called or the police had news about him.

Lily poured a spot of tea into her delicate china cup. "There's always a ranch hand in the yard. And Rosita is just a phone call and a short walk away. So I'll be fine."

Ruben and Rosita Perez lived in a three-bedroom house on the property, which was the only reason Jeremy felt comfortable leaving her to drive into town and volunteer at the clinic. But it wasn't the same as having someone in the house with her, someone to keep her company and make sure she was eating.

"Why don't you invite Maria to join you and Rosita for lunch one of these days?" he suggested.

A slow smile settled across her face. "That's a nice idea. Maybe I should call them tomorrow and set something up."

The clock on the mantel tick-tocked softly, letting them know that it would be bedtime soon.

As Lily lifted her china cup and took a sip, Jeremy asked, "Chamomile?"

She nodded. "I thought it would help me sleep."

They'd both been plagued by insomnia lately, but he

supposed that was to be expected. They had a lot on their minds.

"Are you sure you wouldn't like a little tea or a night-cap to help you unwind?" she asked.

"Not tonight. But thanks."

He set the water on a ceramic, felt-lined coaster and scanned the room, with its traditional Western-style decor. The leather sofas and chairs were fairly new, but the rest of the furniture—the painted armoires, the long oak dining table with high-back chairs, the bookshelves and various pieces of pottery—were antiques that boasted a Spanish influence.

So did the plaster walls, which had been adorned with colorful paintings and hand-woven blankets that had been created by local artisans. One piece in particular had been made by Isabella, J.R.'s wife, and given to Lily as a gift.

Needless to say, J.R. and Isabella's home had been decorated in a similar style, which appealed to Jeremy.

When he first came to Red Rock to celebrate what should have been his father's wedding to Lily, he'd stayed in one of the many guest rooms at J.R.'s ranch. But several weeks after his dad went missing, he'd moved to the Double Crown, hoping to provide Lily with some comfort and support while they waited for William's return.

Six years ago, Lily lost her husband, Ryan, to a brain tumor, and two years later, William was left a widower when Molly died. The surviving spouses had always been friends and had grieved for each other's loss.

Over time, their friendship had deepened, and they gradually fell in love.

Jeremy couldn't have been more pleased to learn of their plan to marry. William and Lily deserved to be happy and to spend their golden years together.

But now, at least for the time being, Lily was alone again, and Jeremy's heart ached for her.

As he sat with her this evening, reflecting on the losses he'd had over the past six years, he wondered if it had been a mistake to pass on a nightcap.

Of course, he hadn't actually lost his dad—not until they found a body—but it was becoming more and more difficult to remain positive that the man would eventually come home, and that the wedding would be rescheduled.

"We'll find him," Lily had said on several different occasions. "I can't explain how I know, but I'm certain he's still alive."

Jeremy took comfort in her quiet faith, and he wondered if Lily might be the one providing support to him, rather than the other way around.

It was possible, he supposed.

There had always been something special about Lily, something that struck Jeremy as both strong and vulnerable at the same time. He wasn't sure what it was about her that he admired the most or what it was that drew him to her, but she provided him with some kind of maternal link that he'd been missing ever since his mom died.

Was that what his dad had come to appreciate about Lily? That she took the edge off his loss, too?

So how was it that Lily held on to hope that William was still alive when even Jeremy was beginning to fear the worst?

Had she experienced a dream or had some kind of premonition?

Under normal circumstances, he wouldn't have asked for an explanation, but his dream and his date with Kirsten were too fresh on his mind, and he found himself quizzing her anyway.

"Can I ask you a question, Lily?"

She glanced up from her teacup and smiled. "Of course."

"Do you ever have dreams that turn out to be real or that might even reveal the future?"

"Why do you ask?"

"Because I had a dream a few nights back. And in it, I saw a woman I'd never met before. I didn't exactly see her face, but I got a glimpse of her hair color and part of her profile. Then, the next day, I met her—or someone who could have been her."

Lily, who still held her teacup, cocked her head slightly to the side. The look in her eyes indicated that she suspected that there was more going on than a chance meeting.

He wouldn't have shared his thoughts about Kirsten and the dream with anyone else, but he trusted Lily with the details. "I had the feeling that I was married in that dream—and that I was happier than I'd ever been before. So when I spotted the woman the next day, it left me a little unbalanced."

"Did you get a chance to talk to her?"

He nodded.

"What's her name?"

"Kirsten."

Lily bent forward and returned her teacup to the saucer that rested on the table. "Maybe you should ask her out."

"Actually," Jeremy said, grinning, "we had dinner together this evening."

Lily blessed him with a slow, knowing smile. "And...?"

"I enjoyed our time together and would like to take her out again."

Lily's smile faded. "Why do I get the feeling that there's a problem?"

"Because I've got a practice in Sacramento and won't be in Red Rock forever."

Silence shrouded the room as they both realized what was keeping him in town. Finally, Lily said, "You've put your life on hold for your father, Jeremy. And I can appreciate that. But are you sure it's not going to affect your practice to be away from it for so long?"

"I took that leave of absence for several reasons," he admitted. "I need some time to reevaluate a few things in my life."

Lily leaned back in her seat and placed her hands in her lap. "And how is Kirsten affecting your reevaluation process?"

"I'm not sure. But if what I'm feeling for her continues

to grow, it's going to… Well, it will certainly complicate my life."

Hell, just meeting her seemed to have complicated his life already.

"This sounds serious," Lily said.

"If you're talking about love, it's way too soon for anything like that. I'm attracted to her, of course, but it's even more than that. She really intrigues me, and I'm drawn to her."

"It sounds like love at first sight to me."

Jeremy slowly shook his head. "No, it can't be that."

"I've been in love twice in my life," Lily said. "So no one knows better than I do how inexplicable that feeling can be."

"It's not *love,*" Jeremy repeated, sure that he couldn't possibly have feelings like that so soon. "I don't even know her."

But if truth be told, he wanted to get to know her a whole lot better—starting tomorrow.

The next day, while Max was out pounding the pavement again and Anthony napped in the Portacrib that served as his bed, Kirsten decided to spend the quiet time unpacking some of the boxes she'd been storing in the hall closet, a chore she'd been putting off ever since she'd moved into the house.

She'd just pulled out a box filled with college textbooks that she hadn't wanted to get rid of, but as she looked through them now, she realized it was silly to keep them. They took up so much space—and they were heavy, too.

Maybe she could donate them to the library or sell them on eBay. As she considered her options for disposing of them, the doorbell rang.

She had no idea who it could be on a weekday afternoon. It was probably a salesman. She'd ignore the person at the door completely, but she was afraid that whoever it was might ring again. And a second chime could wake up the baby, who'd just gone down for a nap and should sleep for a couple hours.

So she got up from the floor, where she'd been kneeling before the box of books, and answered the door.

When she spotted Jeremy on her porch, wearing a pair of black slacks, a pale blue polo shirt and a dazzling smile, her breath caught.

"I hope you don't mind me stopping by unannounced," he said.

Her only concern about his impromptu visit was that it hadn't given her a chance to run a brush through her hair, to put on some lipstick and to change into something other than a UT San Antonio T-shirt and a comfy pair of frayed denim jeans.

But she shook off her momentary embarrassment and said, "Not at all." Then she stepped aside and let him in.

Needless to say, she was surprised to see Jeremy, but the two white bags he carried left her especially curious about why he'd stopped by—in spite of her being glad that he had.

Once she closed the door, she asked, "What's that?"

His eyes glimmered with mirth. "I owed you dessert, remember? So I hope you're hungry."

"You brought *dessert?*" She laughed. "I wasn't going to hold you to it." Again, she studied the bags, awed by the gesture. "What did you do? Buy out a bakery?"

"I didn't have to go that far. I just called Bernardo's and ordered takeout of every dessert they have on the menu, including the chocolate soufflé, which is still warm and supposed to be their specialty."

And he'd brought all of it to *her?*

His efforts were both adorable and mind-boggling. Was this what dating Jeremy Fortune was going to be like?

Not that they were dating, exactly.

Oh, no? a small inner voice asked. *And just what would you call it?*

"Come with me," she said. "I'll get some plates and forks."

He followed her into the small kitchen, where her dinner simmered in a Crock-Pot on the counter, filling the room with the aroma of chicken and vegetables.

"Where do you want me to set this up?" he asked.

Still amazed at his presence, as well as his gesture, she suggested he spread it out on the table, then asked, "Should I put on some coffee? Or would you rather have milk?"

"I'll have whatever you're having." He set the bags on one of the chairs, then proceeded to pull out take-out containers filled with tiramisu, cheesecake, cannoli, a fruit tart, biscotti, fresh berries and what had to be the soufflé he'd mentioned. "I hope you don't mind, but I decided not to bring the gelato. I was afraid it would melt before I got here."

"Believe me," she said, "I don't think we're going to miss the ice cream."

Within minutes, her table looked like a dessert buffet at a wedding. When Jeremy took a step back and smiled at his handiwork, she laughed. "You must have a real sweet tooth, Dr. Fortune."

"I do. But I was also a Boy Scout, and we were taught to be prepared."

"For what?" she asked, chuckling. "A sugar embargo?"

"I wanted to make sure I had whatever you would have ordered last night."

"I probably would have just asked for a bite of whatever you were having," she admitted. What in the world were they going to do with all these goodies?

"Why do women do that?" he asked. "Just ask for a bite when they'd like the whole thing?"

"Because it's a way to diet and have our cake, too." But if Kirsten had any ideas about counting carbs or calories today, she was going to be toast. Because she wanted to try a little of everything he brought.

While she put on a pot of coffee, she couldn't help but wonder just how far a man like Jeremy would go for a woman he cared about, and a smidgen of envy stirred in her heart.

If he didn't have ties to Sacramento, if he was settled here in Red Rock...

As the water began to gurgle and dribble into the carafe, she realized that he'd certainly gone out of his way for her today. Did that mean he cared about her in spite of the reasons a long-lasting relationship between them wasn't feasible?

Or was she just a date he was trying to impress?

No, that couldn't be it. The man was impressive enough in his own right and didn't need to play games like that. Any woman would be lucky to have caught his eye, even if it was just a temporary thing.

After Jeremy set out the plates, silverware and napkins, he wandered over to the Crock-Pot and peered through the glass lid. "Boy, this sure smells good."

"It's just a little something I threw in for dinner."

A part of her wanted to invite him to stay, but Max was so unpredictable these days. She never knew what he'd say or how he'd act. And she wasn't up for the stress. Not when she was hoping this "temporary thing" with Jeremy would last longer than a date or two. So she decided to let the whole thing ride.

When the coffee was finished, she poured two cups. "How do you like yours?" she asked. "Cream? Sugar? Both?"

"Black, thanks."

She added a bit of skim milk and artificial sweetener to hers, which was clearly a waste of time considering the sugar and calories they were about to consume, but she wasn't going to blink an eye at the indulgence. Instead, she joined him at the table.

He took his fork and cut into the tiramisu, then offered the bite to her. "Here, try this."

She opened her mouth, letting him feed her. The sweet, gooey taste was mesmerizing, but she was more awed by the fact that he was spoon-feeding her.

Could anything be sexier than that?

Yes, she realized. If they were feeding each other in bed after making love all afternoon.

"What do you think?" he asked.

About feeding each other in bed? She forced herself to focus on the taste of the tiramisu instead. "It's delicious. You're going to have to try it, too."

Then she reached for a fork, filled it with a man-size portion, and offered it to him. As he opened his mouth, something wild and exciting rushed through her—setting off a vision of the two of them sitting amid tangled sheets, romantic music on the radio, feeling both sated and hungry at the same time...

Enough of that, she told herself. She'd be hungry for a lot more than sweets if she wasn't careful. So she cut into a cannoli—were they really going to keep feeding each other?—and lifted the fork to his lips, offering him another taste and leaving a bit of whipped cream at the edge of his mouth.

She reached out and wiped it away with her finger, but as their gazes locked, his hand grasped her wrist and her movements froze. As his face leaned toward hers, time slowed to a crawl and anticipation filled her to the brim.

If she'd thought their last kiss had been breathtaking, she had a feeling that this one would be all that and more.

And she was right.

As their lips met and parted, his tongue swept inside her mouth, sending a heated rush to the most feminine part of her. She reached toward him, her fingers snaking through his golden-brown locks, drawing him closer and deepening the kiss.

Passion flared, rocking her to the core. She couldn't seem to get enough of him or his sweet, creamy taste. And she realized that if he took her hand, drew her to a stand, swept her into his arms and carried her to the bedroom, she wouldn't have stopped him. She wouldn't have even considered it.

How could anything that started out so sweet and innocent burst into all-consuming desire?

When the kiss finally ended—she wasn't even sure who had come up for air first—her mind scrambled to get a grip on both her hormones and her emotions.

What was going on between them?

Was he feeling it, too—the heat, the passion?

"I didn't come over here to take you to bed," he said.

She almost wished that he had. And while she knew she ought to say something, her heart and mind were still spinning out of control.

As she tried to gather her wits, which seemed to be a

real struggle at the moment, a response to his comment failed her.

"You look a little uneasy," he said.

Heavens, no. She was just a little stunned and shaken, that was all. If this was what his kiss did to her, what would making love with him be like?

"I…" She caught herself before she ended up rambling about how deeply that kiss had affected her, how badly she wanted to share another—and anything else he had in mind. "It just took me by surprise."

"I'm sorry if I was out of line."

"Oh, no. Not at all. It's just that…" She struggled for a moment over how to continue, but why beat around the bush and play games? Opting for honesty, she said, "Well, it was a little earthshaking."

Surely, he'd felt it, too.

A grin splashed across his face. "I'd have to agree with you there."

This was probably the time to invite him to stay to dinner, but as the baby cried out, announcing naptime was over and drawing her back to reality, she couldn't bring herself to do it.

"I…uh…better get Anthony," she said. "He's going to want a bottle."

Talk about lousy timing.

But maybe it was for the best. What she'd just shared with Jeremy had been the kind of thing that dreams were made of. And a fussy baby was sure to put a king-size damper on that.

So could a surly brother, who might walk in at any time.

"Is there something I can do to help?" Jeremy asked.

"Not that I can think of." How could she ask him to fix a bottle of formula or to check on Anthony and see if his diaper was wet—or *worse?*

Talk about being jerked out of the dream world and thrust into reality.

"I've got it," she said, as she excused herself to get the baby.

She just hoped that when she returned, Jeremy wouldn't decide that dating her wouldn't be worth the real-life complications she was sure to toss into the mix.

Chapter Five

Jeremy had never been so turned on by something as simple as a kiss before, especially one in which he and the woman had been fully clothed and seated at a kitchen table.

As Kirsten went into the other room to get the crying baby, he watched the alluring sway of her denim-clad hips, the swish of her honey-brown hair across her shoulders.

She had some kind of a hold on him, although he'd be damned if he knew what it was, and it only seemed to be growing stronger.

He didn't believe in love at first sight, so he knew it wasn't that. Hell, he'd barely had a chance to get to know her, to talk about some of the meatier subjects in life. So whatever he was feeling had to be strictly biological—a mixture of lust, hormones and chemistry.

Or was it more than that?

Either way, there was no getting around the fact that Kirstin would be a dynamite lover. Two kisses had convinced him of that.

So now what? His visit had clearly taken an unexpected turn, and he wasn't sure whether he should stay or go.

He'd clearly surprised her by showing up at her house this afternoon, and while she'd been elbow-deep in some domestic chore and not wearing any makeup to speak of, it hadn't mattered one bit. He still found her beautiful, as well as intriguing. Maybe even more so now.

When she returned to the kitchen with Anthony, he watched as she cuddled the hungry baby while preparing to feed him.

"Need some help?" he asked, even though she seemed to be juggling the infant, a bottle of water and a scoop of powdered formula as if it was all in a day's work.

"Thanks, but I've got it. I have a system that seems to work, even when I'm home alone." She laughed, the lilt of her voice a pleasant sound that played havoc with his senses. "But you should've seen me when Anthony first arrived. I was so inept with this little guy that it was almost funny."

Jeremy found that hard to believe. She certainly looked like a pro as she settled into the kitchen chair and placed the nipple in the baby's mouth.

Anthony quickly latched on and began sucking as though it might be the last bottle he'd ever get.

"Goodness," she said. "Would you look at him go?"

Jeremy was looking all right, but at the whole picture of woman and child. Kirsten was a natural, and he couldn't help picturing her holding *his* baby.

And why would he do that?

He'd never had visions of himself as a father before. Not that he didn't want kids—his life had just been too busy, too complicated, too focused on his medical practice. For as long as he'd been in Sacramento, he hadn't been able to think much beyond the next patient, the next X-ray or the next surgery.

But for some crazy reason, when he was with Kirsten, his entire focus shifted to another level. There was just something about her, about being with her, that made him feel…different.

In some ways, she reminded him of his mom, and he wondered if Kirsten had a playful side, too.

Molly Fortune had adored her five sons, but she hadn't been a pushover. She'd made them each toe the mark. Still, she'd known how to play with them, how to laugh and enjoy their company. And that had made for a happy childhood and a heart filled with memories.

Would Kirsten, like Jeremy's mom, be the playful kind of mother who would help her kids build a tree house in the backyard? Would she lead a Cub Scout troop? And on rainy days, would she help them build a fortress in the living room out of sheets and blankets?

Not all mothers would.

And why should it even matter?

Hell if he knew. Although he suspected that it might be due to the fact that he'd been so studious in school, so driven to get a medical degree, so focused on his career, that he was finally ready to kick back, have some fun and enjoy himself for a change.

Before his mom had died, she'd taken him aside and said, "I'm glad to see you working so hard, honey. But I worry about you. There's so much more to life than work. You really need to take time to play."

Jeremy hadn't taken her seriously at the time, but he wished he had. Her words were just now beginning to sink in.

He watched Kirsten for a moment or two longer, then asked, "Can you get a babysitter on Friday night?" He wouldn't just assume that Max would be around every evening.

"That won't be a problem. Why?"

"I'd like to take you out."

"All right." She smiled, letting him know that the suggestion appealed to her.

"Dress warmly," he said.

Her eyes lit up. "Okay. Where are we going?"

He was just about to tell her, then decided to keep it to himself. "It's a surprise."

A grin splashed across her face. "I love surprises."

Apparently, so did he. Because picking up Kirsten and whisking her off on a fun-filled adventure suddenly sounded like one of the best ideas he'd ever had.

* * *

As Max bent over and peered into the refrigerator, looking for a soda, he scrunched his face at all the take-out containers. "What the heck is all this crap doing in here?"

"It's not crap," Kirsten said, as she stood near the sink and poured out the remaining coffee from the carafe. "It's leftover dessert."

He pulled a cola from the fridge and popped the top. "Left over from what?"

"Jeremy had to cut our date short last night, and since we weren't able to stay long enough to eat dessert, he brought all of that by this afternoon."

"You've gotta be kidding." Max slowly shook his head, still standing in front of the open refrigerator. "Don't you think that's a little over-the-top?"

Actually, she thought it was sweet. But it was clear that Max wouldn't agree. So choosing not to argue, she ignored the fact that Jeremy's visit and thoughtfulness had struck a raw nerve in her brother and asked, "Do you want some cheesecake? It's really good."

"I don't want any of that stuff." Max slammed the refrigerator door a little too hard. "I still haven't figured out what that guy's up to."

"He just came by to see me, that's all."

Max chuffed and slowly shook his head.

"Obviously, you don't like him." Kirsten crossed her arms and braced herself for whatever unfounded objections Max might have. "Why is that? He's an orthopedic surgeon. And a darn good one, from what I've learned by doing a Google search. On top of that, his family is not only well-known, but well respected in Red Rock. Have you ever heard of the Fortune Foundation?"

"Who hasn't?" Max leaned against the refrigerator. "Those people think they own the town."

If Kirsten had a violent streak and lacked self-control, she might have punched her brother's lights out. As it was, she disposed of the old coffee grounds and rinsed out the carafe.

"Open your eyes," Max said. "That guy's just trying to snowball you, sis. And, apparently, it's working."

Kirsten shut off the water, set the clean carafe on the counter and turned to face him. "What are you talking about?"

"He's just trying to score, that's all. I heard that he's only visiting in town. He's going to be moving away soon, and then where will that leave you?"

Kirsten might be dating Jeremy, but that didn't mean she would shut down her radar and jump into a relationship that wasn't in her best interest—at least, not knowingly. She also knew that a lot of men weren't looking for something permanent and long-lasting, that some of them only wanted sex. Shoot, she'd met a couple of them and had been disappointed enough times to take things slow and to be careful.

She was also fully aware of the fact that Jeremy would go back to Sacramento one of these days.

But she was a big girl and didn't need her brother telling her what to do.

For Pete's sake, his own radar had certainly been

faulty or nonexistent when he'd first hooked up with Courtney. But rather than let him draw her into another argument that was sure to escalate without solving anything, she decided to calmly end the conversation and put him in his place.

"Jeremy and I are friends," she said. "But even if we were more than that, I'd like to remind you that this is my house and that I'm a responsible adult."

Max's face reddened and he pursed his lips. Kirsten had never seen steam come out of anyone's ears before, unless it had been in a cartoon on television, but she wouldn't have been surprised to see little cloudlike puffs coming out of her brother's head.

What did he have against Jeremy?

The first time they'd met, Max had scowled all the way home from the medical center. And he'd clearly been a grump when she and Jeremy had left the house to go to Bernardo's last night.

Now this. You'd think Max was a jealous boyfriend rather than an overprotective brother. And quite frankly, he was pushing her to her limit. If it weren't for Anthony, she'd ask him to pack up and move out tonight. As it was, she bit her tongue.

But living with Max was *so* not working.

"You were out of line for entertaining him at the house when Anthony was in the next room," he added.

"Excuse me?" Her voice rose a couple decibels in spite of her determination to remain cool and in control. "You're overreacting." She blew out an exasperated sigh.

"Anthony is an infant, and he was sleeping for most of the time."

Again, she wanted to remind her brother that she was an adult. And that he was...

Heck, who even knew what he was. For a twenty-six-year-old man, acting mature seemed like a real struggle for him some days.

"Did you kiss him?" Max asked.

Before responding and putting her brother in his place, she took another calming breath, then slowly let it out. "That's none of your business."

He remained silent for a while, as though her words had finally sunk in. Then he said, "I'm sorry, Kirsten. You're right."

His acquiescence surprised her, and she waited for him to interject a "but" to the conversation.

Instead, he said, "I guess I was out of line."

He *guessed?*

"It's just that I don't like to be reminded that you're the responsible one, when I've been trying my best to find a job—*any* job. And to make matters worse, I've got a lot on my mind."

She sighed. "I know you do. Having another human being who is dependent upon you must be stressful, especially while you're out of work."

"It's not just that..." He paused, as if trying to find the words to explain what was really bothering him and why he'd been lashing out at her and Jeremy.

"Then what is it?" she asked. Was her brother missing Courtney? Was he feeling badly that Kirsten might be involved in a budding romance when his own relationship with the mother of his son had fallen apart?

Finally, Max said, "I've got things to deal with that you wouldn't understand."

"Share them with me. Let me help. We're family."

He clammed up, refusing to elaborate any further.

She could have prodded him, she supposed. He was clearly bothered by something and lashing out at her because of it. But spending so much of her energy sympathizing with Max was getting old, and she was just plain tired of dealing with all the problems resulting from his bad decisions.

For as long as she could remember, she'd been both mother and father to him, a role that was slowly wearing her down, especially since Max had such a bad attitude about anything she did or said to help him—unless it was handing him cash in silence.

She would have to resort to tough love again, which had worked well in the past, but now there was the baby to consider.

It was comforting to know that Max had taken on the responsibility of fatherhood, but that didn't stop her from worrying.

As much as she'd tried to convince herself that he was able to handle the baby on his own, she had to admit that she had her doubts.

At a quarter to noon the next day, Jeremy was reviewing an X-ray of an elderly patient. He tried to focus on the scans before him, but in the back of his mind, he couldn't help thinking about Kirsten and wondering if she'd like to have lunch with him.

They had a date tomorrow night, something sure to surprise her, but he wanted to see her sooner than that. So he picked up his cell phone and gave her a call.

She answered on the second ring, and when he told her what he had in mind for today, she said, "Lunch sounds great, but Max is out job hunting again, and I've got Anthony."

"Then why don't I bring the food to you?" he asked.

He could almost hear the smile in her voice. "I'd like that, Jeremy."

"How about turkey sandwiches?"

"That's perfect. I'll have beverages to choose from, some fruit and…" She laughed. "Well, don't bother picking up dessert, either. I've still got leftovers."

Twenty minutes later, Jeremy took a midday break from the clinic and showed up on Kirsten's front stoop with the lunch he'd picked up from the deli.

She'd been expecting him, so it was no wonder that she'd applied a coat of lipstick and had brushed her hair to a glossy shine. But it was her bright-eyed smile that did him in, reaching deep into his chest and turning him inside out.

As she stepped aside to let him into the cozy living room, he spotted the baby in a stroller.

"Going somewhere?" he asked.

"If you're up for a walk." There it went again, that smile and that single dazzling dimple, and he realized he'd be up for just about anything with her.

"There's a community park about a block down the street," she explained. "And the sun's out today. Why don't we take a walk and have a picnic?"

"Sounds like fun."

And Jeremy hadn't had fun in ages.

"I've got some iced tea and goodies packed and ready to go." She reached for a cooler that was on the floor, next to the sofa.

"Here, let me carry that." He took the handle from her. "You'll have your hands full with the stroller."

As they left the house, and she locked the door behind them, he let her direct him to the park. February weather could always be a little iffy, but she'd been right. It was sunny today. And he could see why she'd want to get out of the house.

"What would you have done if I didn't want to picnic?" he asked.

Her blue eyes glistened. "I figured a man who liked surprises wouldn't mind eating in the park."

Once he'd reached adulthood, Jeremy had never really liked surprises, at least not until meeting Kirsten. For some reason, he found himself thinking about things that would be new, fun and exciting. But there was no need to let something like that out the bag. Besides, he didn't care where they had lunch, as long as they were together.

They walked several blocks to a small grassy area that wasn't much more than a playground with a couple picnic tables, but it would do. And since it was a school day, they had the place to themselves.

Kirsten parked the stroller next to one of the tables, in the shade of a tree. Then she set out their meal: the sandwiches, fresh fruit, iced tea and cheesecake. Since Jeremy only had an hour before he had to get back to the clinic, they took their seats and began to eat.

It was easy to talk to Kirsten, who was a good listener. And before he knew it, he was telling her about his morning, about an elderly patient with a broken hip and a boy who'd fractured his arm during morning recess.

She leaned toward him as he talked and listened intently while he shared details that might be boring to someone else.

As the sun shone down on them, as a cool breeze whispered through the leaves in the trees, he realized it would be nice coming home to someone like her every day. But it had only been days since they'd met, so it was way too soon to be thinking about things like commitments and the future. And for that reason, a change in subject was in order.

"How's your brother's job hunt going?" he asked. "Does he have any interviews scheduled?"

"I'm afraid he hasn't had much luck at all." She set down her sandwich and reached for an apple slice.

Jeremy couldn't say that he was surprised. A man's attitude had a lot to do with finding a position with a solid company.

"I might be wrong," he said, "but your brother seems to have a big chip on his shoulder."

"You're right about that. He really hasn't been a happy person for a long time."

"Why?"

"I'm sure it has to do with the bad choices he's made, but he won't do anything to correct them. And to make matters worse, he seems to think that I look down on him."

It would be hard not to, Jeremy thought.

"Don't get me wrong," Kirsten said. "I love my brother and want the best for him. But he seems to have a little gray rain cloud following him all the time. And he can't seem to steer clear of it."

"He's old enough to know when to get out of the rain," Jeremy said.

"I know. I just wish he would work as hard as I did to overcome the strikes we had against us while growing up."

"What kind of strikes?" Jeremy asked, sorry to hear that Kirsten's childhood hadn't been as happy as his had been.

"Our dad left home when I was fourteen." She glanced down at her half-eaten sandwich, then back to Jeremy. "It was tough on me, but Max was only twelve at the time, and he took it especially hard. He acted out as an adolescent, getting into more than the usual amount of trouble, and eventually, he dropped out of school."

The teenage years could be tough, Jeremy realized, even under the best circumstances.

"Our mom had to work two jobs to support us, so I looked after Max and helped him pick up the pieces of his life." Kirsten rewrapped the untouched half of her sandwich and put it in the cooler. "Well, at least I tried to."

Jeremy had a feeling she was taking too much personal responsibility for her brother's failures, and he hated to see her do that. Unable to help himself, he reached out and placed his hand on her forearm. "Max is a big boy now, Kirsten. And as much as you'd like to, you can't keep bailing him out."

"You're right. But I also know what he's been through in the past, so it's hard not to be sympathetic." As her gaze met Jeremy's, he could see the very heart of her in those expressive blue eyes.

Did Max have any idea how lucky he was to have Kirsten in his corner? Jeremy wasn't so sure.

"When my mom died in a car accident five years ago, Max was just getting his life back on track. He'd started attending the adult school, planning to get his GED. But after the funeral, he turned to his friends for support."

He read into what she was really saying; Max had turned away from Kirsten.

"My brother didn't always choose the right friends," she added. "And as a result, he just couldn't seem to stay out of trouble. Of course, it was nothing terrible. But he partied too much on weekends and couldn't keep a job."

"So you've been keeping him afloat ever since?" Jeremy asked.

"For the most part. We received a moderate, wrongful-death settlement after the accident, which was enough for me to put a down payment on my house and to stick some money away for a rainy day. But Max blew through his share. Three years ago, he asked me to loan him money for a car."

"Did you?" Jeremy asked, hoping she hadn't.

"I had to. How was he going to keep his job without one?"

"But he didn't keep it," Jeremy said, connecting the dots.

"No, he didn't. So he couldn't pay his rent, either. And since I'd cosigned on his lease… Well, I had to help out with that, too." She tucked a strand of hair behind her ear. "I finally had enough and told him he was on his own."

"How did he take it?"

"All right, I guess. He hooked up with a girl named Courtney—Anthony's mother—and for a while, everything seemed to be on the uphill swing."

"So cutting him off actually helped?"

"Apparently so. When he and Courtney split up, I expected him to go off the deep end again, but he didn't."

"He kept his job?"

She nodded. "Like I told you before, he really enjoyed working at the feed store. He has a thing for horses and animals. So the layoff hit him hard, and I know he's hurting because of it." She glanced at the stroller, where the baby napped in the shade. "And now there's Anthony to worry about."

Maybe so, but Jeremy could see the writing on the wall, even if Kirsten couldn't. Max needed to make his own way for a change.

"The weird thing is," Kirsten said, "my brother needs my help, but at the same time, he resents it."

Jeremy wondered if Max had finally turned the corner, if he would settle down once he found the right job. He hoped so. It sounded as if Kirsten could use a break.

"What about you?" he asked. "You mentioned being out of work, too."

"Yes, but that's just temporary. I've never had trouble finding or keeping a job. I'm good at what I do, and I've got a great résumé and letters of recommendation, so it's only a matter of time."

"I'm sure you're right," he said, thinking about the clinic and the Fortune Foundation. "I have plenty of connections in town. Maybe I can talk to someone and put in a good word for you."

"Thanks," she said. "That's nice of you, but I really want to get a job on my own merits. It's important to me."

He had to admire her for that. And he couldn't help studying her from across the table, amazed how the sunshine highlighted the golden strands in her hair, how it picked up flecks of green in her pretty blue eyes, making them almost turquoise in color.

If he had the rest of the day at his disposal, he might have enjoyed more time with her, but as it was, he glanced at his wristwatch instead.

"You know," he said, "I'm going to have to call it a day. I need to get back to the clinic."

Kirsten stood, gathered the leftover food and placed

it back in the cooler. "Do you have a full schedule this afternoon?"

"Not that I know of, but that can change from minute to minute." Jeremy tossed the used napkins into the trash receptacle, then gripped the handle of the cooler. "Thanks for suggesting that we have a picnic. It's been a long time since I've done something like this."

And even longer that he'd enjoyed kicking back and just being with a beautiful woman.

"A change in routine keeps life interesting," she said.

His mother used to say things like that. In fact, that was one reason she'd let her sons go to Texas each summer and spend time on the Double Crown Ranch with Ryan and Lily. She had wanted them to have an opportunity to experience another way of life and to gain a broader perspective.

As Kirsten pushed the stroller toward the sidewalk, Jeremy joined her, and they made their way to the street on which she lived.

It was a short walk to the house, yet Jeremy found himself walking slower than he ought to and talking about a memory he'd had while exploring a swimming hole he and his brothers had found near the ranch.

"One day, we decided to go skinny-dipping," he said. "But a couple girls, who'd come with their mother to visit Lily, found us and ran off with our clothes. We stayed in that water until we turned into prunes and had no choice but to go home naked."

"Were the girls still there?" she asked.

"Yes, but lucky for us, we found one of the ranch hands in the barn, and he got us something to wear into the house."

"Now that kind of ranch life had to have been a real change of routine." Kirsten turned to him and grinned, revealing eyes sparking with mirth and a smile a man could get used to seeing.

"It was also a lot of fun. In fact, there were times when each of us pondered the idea of becoming cowboys when we grew up."

"What made you decide to become a doctor?" Kirsten asked.

"I was probably ten when the idea first hit me," Jeremy said. "My older brothers and I had been playing in a tree house in our backyard. Nick was climbing up the steps and horsing around with J.R. who was right below him. In the process, Nick lost his balance, fell and broke his arm. It was a compound fracture, and I remember seeing the way the bone jutted out of his skin."

"So his injury inspired you?" she asked.

"It was definitely the first time the thought crossed my mind. I felt sorry for Nick, of course. I knew he was in a lot of pain. But I begged my mom to let me go to the E.R. with them, and for some reason, she gave in. I found the whole hospital experience fascinating and quizzed the orthopedic surgeon until he probably wanted to tape my mouth shut." Jeremy chuckled, looking back on it all from the perspective of an adult.

"I wish I could say that I had an epiphany like that

when I decided on my career," Kirsten said. "But I didn't."

"So why did you choose to become an accountant?" he asked, thinking that she was a natural-born caretaker and might have made a good teacher or even a nurse.

"I've always been good at math, so bookkeeping seemed like the field to study. Looking back, I think that I was drawn to a career like that because it provides order and structure in my life."

Something told him that was because her brother provided so much instability to her life, and at least the laws of math and accounting were constant.

Jeremy couldn't help wondering if there was something he could say to her brother, something he could do to help him get back on track. He had a feeling it would make Kirsten's life a lot easier.

When they reached her house, where Jeremy had left his car parked at the curb, Max was arriving at the same time and parked his small white pickup in the driveway— probably the vehicle his sister had helped him buy.

Max appeared to be in a slightly better mood than before, which made Jeremy think that maybe he'd been wrong about the guy after all.

"How did it go today?" Kirsten asked her brother.

Max shrugged, his expression more of a scowl when he turned her way.

If Jeremy had more time, he'd take Max aside and maybe ask him to join him for a beer. A man-to-man talk might go a long way. But then again, maybe he was only barking up the wrong tree.

Either way, he had to get back to the clinic.

"I'll talk to you later," Jeremy told Kirsten. He was tempted to kiss her goodbye but chose not to in front of Max.

"Okay." She smiled, and he wondered if the same thought had crossed her mind, as well as the same decision. "Have a good afternoon."

"You, too."

As Jeremy opened the car door and slid behind the wheel, he overheard Max tell his sister, "Looks like this is becoming a habit."

Jeremy wasn't sure what he meant by that, but there was a lot of truth to it, he supposed.

For some reason, Kirsten Allen had become habit-forming—and one that might prove difficult to break.

Chapter Six

"What were you and the doctor doing?" Max asked Kirsten, as he followed her into the living room. "Playing house?"

Her hands tightened on the grip of the stroller's handle, as she shot a look of disbelief at her brother.

Just moments ago, he'd made a comment about them seeing each other becoming a habit, something she was sure Jeremy had overheard. She'd been embarrassed but had to let it go until she could confront Max when they were alone. So she'd bitten her tongue and taken Anthony into the house.

But she wouldn't hold back any longer. "You're *way* out of line, Max."

"On, come on. You've been hearing wedding bells and dreaming of having a baby of your own since you were a little girl. First you pretended to be my mother when we were kids. And now you're pretending to be Anthony's."

Heat blasted her cheeks as she listened to his false accusations and pondered the absurdity of it all. Sure, she'd played with dolls as a girl. And she'd set them aside when her little brother was born, preferring to cuddle and play with the real thing instead.

But so what? Most little girls who'd been given a baby brother would have happily taken on a role like that. And the fact that Max was implying she had some kind of weird psychological need to...

Oh, for crying out loud, she had no idea *what* he was getting at, but she no longer cared.

"That's it." She parked the stroller near the sofa, turned on her heel and slapped her hands on her hips. "I've had it."

His eye twitched, but he didn't back down.

And neither did she. "Let's get one thing straight, Max. I'm sick and tired of mothering you—no matter what you might think."

"Good," he finally said, although his voice lacked its previous bluster.

"And as for Anthony, he's a precious little baby who needs a mother, since the one who left him here obviously doesn't have a maternal bone in her body. So you should be thanking your lucky stars that I'm willing to be his aunt and help you out."

Her brother's shoulders slumped ever so slightly, although he kept his chin up.

Anthony began to fuss, no doubt preparing for a full-on you-woke-me-up wail. But rather than go to him, gently pick him up and shush him, as had become her habit this past week, she let him cry.

"Your son needs you," she said. "He's due for a diaper change and a bottle. And you're on duty now."

"That's fine."

Kristen strode across the room and retrieved her purse, which was on the shelf near the stairs. After slipping the strap over her shoulder, she headed for the door.

"Where are you going?" he asked.

As she reached for the doorknob, she paused long enough to look over her shoulder and say, "I haven't decided. But I can assure you that I plan to enjoy the rest of my day—alone and free of any family responsibilities."

Then she left the house.

The breeze kicked up a strand of her hair and blew it across her face, but she merely brushed it aside. After climbing behind the wheel of her car, she started the engine and headed to town.

She wasn't sure just what she'd do there. Something unexpected and sure to make her feel better, she supposed.

If she were a woman from another generation, she might buy herself a new hat.

Now that was an interesting idea. She rarely indulged in shopping trips, and while she'd made it a point to curtail her spending until she landed another job and started receiving regular paychecks, she wasn't going to worry about the expense right now. She had a credit card she rarely used and always paid off, so it was free from debt.

Besides, she had a date with Jeremy on Friday—and she wanted something new to wear.

"Dress warmly," he'd told her.

She had no idea what he had in mind, but she decided to splurge on a new outfit. After all, if things worked out the way she hoped they would, the two of them would be going out again—maybe even regularly.

Deep down she knew she might be putting more stock in her budding relationship than she ought to. But she needed Jeremy in her life at a time like this, even if she couldn't count on having him around later. He was so levelheaded, so wise, so easy to talk to, that she wanted to enjoy every opportunity she had with him.

As thoughts of Jeremy swept over her, she relived each heated kiss they'd shared, as well as the rush of desire that had swept through her whenever they touched, whenever she caught a hint of his woodsy cologne.

Maybe, while out shopping, she ought to consider getting some new lingerie—the slinky kind one might find at Victoria's Secret.

Talk about looking forward to their next date.

As she turned onto the highway that led to the Red Rock shopping district, a niggle of insecurity burrowed deep within her, setting her on edge.

Jeremy was a nice guy—a doctor who was seeing low-income patients at the clinic out of the goodness of his heart. He'd make a fine catch for any woman, but why her?

Why would their chance meeting in a parking lot lead to romance?

He'd also offered to put in a good word for her around town and help with her job search. Was he trying to "fix" her, just like he would set a broken bone?

She tried to shrug off the momentary lack of confidence, instead choosing to believe that Jeremy truly had feelings for her, that he wanted to help because he was a caring person and being helpful was part of his nature.

Don't get your hopes up, she told herself. Their relationship, whatever it was or might become, was only temporary. And they both knew it.

Besides, he came from a nice family—the Fortunes, for goodness' sake. They wouldn't be used to the kind of drama Max always put her through. Would it be enough to chase him off?

She certainly hoped not. She'd told him a lot of stuff already. Maybe it would be best to hold her tongue from here on out. To keep Max and his woes to herself.

That might be wise if she wanted something to develop between them.

But did she?

As tempting as it might be to throw caution to the wind and experience a wild and wonderful romantic relationship with Jeremy for as long as it lasted, she couldn't help worrying that she might be setting herself up for heartbreak.

After all, if she let herself go and fell for him, saying

goodbye and having him leave Red Rock might shake her very foundation.

And then where would she be?

Yet in spite of her apprehension, she couldn't help daydreaming about becoming Dr. Fortune's wife.

And wondering what it would be like to have a baby with him someday.

After Jeremy returned to the clinic, he put in a couple hours at work, first consulting with one of the pediatricians on a suspicious break that was clearly a case of child abuse and then turning in his report to a social worker. Next he talked to a sixty-two-year-old man about the advantages of a knee replacement. Despite the long consultations, his afternoon ended earlier than usual.

On his way back to the Double Crown Ranch, he stopped by the Fortune Foundation, a nonprofit organization that had been founded in Ryan Fortune's memory.

Since Ryan had always believed in paying it forward, it had seemed only fitting to create a charitable organization that helped others in need. And Jeremy was proud of the work they did.

The three-story brick building, which had a day-care center on the ground floor and a playground in back, was located on the highway, just outside of town.

It was after four o'clock when Jeremy entered the lobby and took the elevator to the third floor, hoping to find Nick, his older brother.

At thirty-nine, Nick, the second born of William Fortune's children, was a financial analyst for the foundation. And he'd never been happier.

Jeremy couldn't help thinking about all the changes there'd been in Nick's life these past two years.

Once a confirmed bachelor, he'd become a guardian of triplets. The baby girls eventually wound up in the custody of their aunt and uncle, but not before Nick fell head over heels in love with Charlene London, their nanny.

Now Nick and Charlene had a baby of their own, a cute little boy named Matthew, with red hair, green eyes and a splash of freckles, just like his beautiful mother.

As the elevator doors opened, Jeremy stepped into the lobby, where an attractive young woman with long brown hair sat behind a desk. He didn't remember meeting her before and assumed she was new.

"Hello, there," she said, in a soft, Southern drawl. "You look lost. Can I help you?"

He'd known exactly where he was going, although he'd been deep in thought. But he couldn't see any point in chatting with the woman. He was here to see his brother.

"I'm looking for Nick Fortune," he responded. "Is he available?"

"I'll check and see. He's been in and out all day." Her gaze scanned the length of Jeremy, as though checking him out. Then she slowly got up and walked around her desk.

She was wearing a stylish black top, with a neckline that might be a smidgen low for an office job, a bright turquoise skirt and a pair of high heels that set off shapely legs. She was, Jeremy admitted, a very attractive woman—probably in her early twenties. Not that he was interested.

"I can let Nick know that you're here," she said.

Yet she continued to study him as though he were a chocolate éclair in a bakery window, leaving him feeling a little awkward.

"And your name is…?" she asked.

"Jeremy."

Her smile nearly lit the room as she instigated a hand-shake. "My name's Wendy. I'm an administrative assistant with the Fortune Foundation. Is there anything I can do for you?"

"I'm afraid not."

She paused for a beat, her frown a bit pouty, reminding him of a Southern belle who'd been used to getting her way over the years.

Then she reached across the desk for the telephone receiver. As she did so, her bend-and-stretch motion caused her skirt to hike up and reveal a shapely length of upper leg.

He couldn't help wondering if her movement had been deliberate, but before he could decide—and before she could page Nick—a door swung open.

Jeremy turned toward the sound and spotted his brother, who was wearing his customary business-casual attire, tortoiseshell glasses and spiky brown hair.

"Hey," Nick said, picking up his pace as he approached the lobby. "It's good to see you, Doc."

Wendy returned the telephone receiver to the cradle, leaned against her desk and crossed her arms.

"I see you two have met," Nick said, glancing first at Jeremy, then at his assistant.

"Not really." A slow smile spread across Wendy's pretty face as she looked at Jeremy.

"Meet Wendy Fortune," Nick said. "She's from the Atlanta branch of the family and new to Red Rock."

"It's nice to be formally introduced," the young woman said.

"Jeremy's my brother," Nick explained. "He's visiting from Sacramento and staying with Lily out on the Double Crown."

Wendy's smile faded, but she quickly recovered and laughed. "Another cousin? It seems as if every handsome man who walks into the Fortune Foundation ends up bein' a relative of mine."

"Not all of them," Nick said, before asking her if he had any messages.

Wendy straightened, reached for a sheet of paper on her desk and handed it to him. "Mr. Landers called. And so did your wife. But she said it wasn't important. She wanted you to pick up somethin' on your way home."

"Thanks." Nick nodded toward his office. "Let's go and talk where it's quiet. It's been a busy day."

Moments later, Jeremy had taken a seat across from his brother's desk.

"What do you think of our new hire?" Nick asked.

Jeremy shrugged. "She's a little flashy, I suppose. But if she can do the job…"

"That's just it. I'm not sure if she can—or how serious she is about being here—not just at the foundation, but in Red Rock. Her father called last month, asking if we could put her to work as a favor to him. She's the youngest of six kids and dropped out of college a couple months ago. Her dad's a little exasperated with her, and he's hoping that a move to Texas and a job with the Fortune Foundation will give her some direction in life."

"How's it working out?"

"I don't know. All right, I suppose. She's got a good heart, but she's clearly more interested in striking up a romance than in looking for productive things to do."

"She *was* a little flirty," Jeremy said.

"A *little?*" Nick laughed. "Didn't you see the way she zeroed in on you?"

"Truthfully?" Jeremy slowly shook his head. "I really wasn't paying that much attention to her."

"You must have a lot on your mind, then."

He did—a beautiful accountant who had him tied up in knots.

"Is there anything I can do to help?" Nick asked.

"I just came by to pick your brain. I'm looking for a program of some kind that would help a high school dropout get his GED."

Jeremy was hoping to encourage Max to continue his education in the evenings. Of course, he was doing it mostly for Kirsten. The less she had to worry about when it came to Max and his welfare, the easier her life was going to be.

Nick reached for his iPhone and searched the files.

Then he made a note for Jeremy on a yellow sticky note. "Here's the name and contact information for the woman who's in charge of the adult education department at the local high school. She'll be able to answer all your questions."

"Thanks." Jeremy studied the number he would call as soon as he got back into the car. "I'm also going to need information about day-care options, especially for an infant."

When Kirsten went back to work, Max would need to find someone to watch Anthony for him.

"We offer day care on the first floor," Nick said. "But I'm not sure of the age requirement. When you go downstairs, stop by the director's office."

"All right, I will."

Nick sat back in his chair. "So who are you trying to help?"

"Just a friend."

Jeremy must have gotten a dreamy look in his eyes while thinking of Kirsten, because Nick straightened, leaned forward and placed his hands on the desk. "Is this a *lady* friend?"

"Why do you ask?"

"Because Wendy's pretty hot. And you didn't give her the time of day. Even before you knew she was our cousin."

Apparently, Nick had seen clear through him. But then again, he always had.

"It's just a woman I'm seeing. I'm not sure where it's going yet."

"Sounds like she could complicate your life—hopefully, in a nice way."

Jeremy merely smiled.

She already had.

When Jeremy got to Kirsten's house on Friday night, he knew he was arriving a little earlier than the time they'd agreed upon. So he had a feeling she might not be ready to go.

But he hadn't expected her to be gone.

"She went to the grocery store to pick up formula and disposable diapers," Max said, stepping aside to let Jeremy into the living room. "She shouldn't be too long."

Jeremy tried to read the younger man's expression, but wasn't having much luck. Still, he didn't seem to be as irritable this evening as he'd been on other occasions.

Deciding to tell him what he'd been up to—and what was on his mind—Jeremy said, "I'm not sure if you found a job yet, but I know of a ranch that's looking for a hand. Is that something you'd be interested in doing?"

Whatever had masked Max's expression earlier slipped away, leaving him wide-open and easy to read now, as surprise and disbelief washed over him and hope flickered in his eyes. "Sure, I'd really like working on a ranch."

"It's out on the Double Crown," Jeremy said, "which is a great place for you to get some training and experience. That is, if you want to learn and are willing to work hard."

"Are you kidding? The Double Crown is hiring?"

Well, they weren't actually looking for ranch hands. But knowing that Max had enjoyed his work at the feed store and that he had experience working with feed and grain, as well as animals and supplies, Jeremy had taken a gamble.

He'd also decided to trust that Kirsten's instincts about her brother had been right. So after first talking it over with Lily and getting her okay, he'd gone to see Ruben Perez, the foreman. They'd both agreed to take a chance on Max—as a favor to Jeremy.

Noticing Jeremy's hesitant expression, Max, who'd brightened at first, stiffened and reeled in his initial excitement. "I don't need a handout."

"I'm sure you don't. But I'd heard you enjoyed working at the feed lot. I just assumed working on a ranch might be something you'd be interested in."

Max paused briefly, clearly stewing over the possibility, then said, "I would like it. But why are you trying to help me?"

"I'm not, I guess. The ranch needs a good hand. And you're looking for a job. I just thought it might be a win-win for both of us. But it's not a big deal."

Max thought about it a moment, then softened. "Actually, it's a really big deal. And I'd like to apply—if they're accepting applications."

"It hasn't even gone that far yet," Jeremy said. "When I heard about the opening, I put in a good word for you. It's yours if you want it."

Max furrowed his brow, then cocked his head to

the side as if stumped at how to react. Finally, he said, "Thanks. I really appreciate that."

Jeremy had called in a favor, but that was as far as it would go. From here on out, Max would need to prove himself. "You won't let me down, will you?"

"Absolutely not." Max, who was still clearly reeling from the news, slowly shook his head in awe.

Just watching the transformation in his attitude had been worth Jeremy's efforts.

"Wow," Max said, as he raked a hand through his light brown hair and blew out a sigh. "This is so cool. It's hard to wrap my mind around it. Things like this just don't happen to me."

"Maybe your luck has turned. And now all you have to do is your part."

"Oh, I will," Max said. "You can count on that."

"There's just one thing," Jeremy added.

"What's that?"

"The position is only part-time and temporary to begin with, but it could work into something permanent."

"That's okay," Max said. "I'll work my ass off to prove to them—and to *you*—that I deserve a full-time position. I'd do *anything* to work on a ranch like that one."

"Anything?" Jeremy asked.

"Absolutely."

A slow smile stretched across Jeremy's face. "I'm glad to hear that."

"Why? What's the catch?"

"Because I heard that you don't have a high school diploma, and one of the Double Crown job requirements will be to enroll in an adult education program. There's one in Red Rock that offers a GED program, but they also have classes in animal husbandry. There's a lot to learn when working on a ranch—and the Double Crown is looking for experienced hands and prefers to offer them long-term employment. But they're willing to give a hardworking, dedicated guy a try."

"I don't know about school, though." Max glanced down at the scuffed toes of his shoes and scrunched his face. When he looked up at Jeremy, apprehension peered through his eyes, revealing a frightened little boy who'd been hurt and disappointed time and again. "I mean, I'll *sign up* and all. That's not the problem. It's just that I'm not sure how good I'll do. I've never liked sitting at a desk in a classroom, mostly because I've probably got attention deficit disorder or something that never got diagnosed. But I'll definitely give it my best shot."

"That's all that matters, Max. You just need to do your best."

The younger man seemed to give that some thought, but only for a beat. "Okay. When do I start?"

"I'd like to pick you up tomorrow morning and drive you out to the Double Crown so I can introduce you to Ruben Perez, your boss. And he can give you a job description and let you know when he wants you to work. Then on Monday morning, you can register for classes." He'd also looked into the day care his brother had recommended and found out it had a sliding scale fee structure, but he'd bring that up later.

"Wow," Max said again. "This is too awesome for words. I don't know how to thank you, Dr. Fortune."

"First of all, just do your best—on the ranch and in the classroom. And secondly, don't call me *Doctor*. I'm Jeremy to you."

Max tossed him a crooked grin, clearly humbled and pleased.

"There's one last thing," Jeremy added. "I hope you take this in the spirit in which its given—I want you to be respectful of your sister, even if you think she's wrong or off base."

Max reached out his hand. "You've got yourself a deal."

As they shook on it, something told Jeremy that Max was going to be a whole lot more pleasant to be around from now on, and that Kirsten was in for a big surprise when she saw the metamorphosis.

"You know," Max said, "I've got to tell you something. I love my sister—I really do. And I don't mean to be disrespectful. She's helped me out a lot over the years, but I beat myself up all the time about a lot of the dumb things I've done in the past, and when she starts in on me... Well, it makes me feel like a stupid little kid." He glanced at the portable crib, where Anthony slept. "And now that I'm a father... Damn. It really scares the crap out of me when I think about letting my son down—like my old man did to me."

"Sometimes an honest chat about what's really going on can help a lot," Jeremy said.

"You're probably right." Max pointed to the sofa. "Why don't you sit down. I'm not sure what's keeping Kirsten, but I'm sure she'll be here soon."

As Jeremy settled into his seat, Max said, "I need to apologize to you. I was kind of a jerk when we first met, and I'm sorry about that."

Jeremy could have brushed it off and made it easy on him, but maybe it was best if Max thought twice about the way he treated people in the future. "I figured you didn't want your sister to have a…" What? A boyfriend? A date? "…another guy in her life."

"It's not that. It's just that…" Max took a deep breath, as if needing a shot of oxygen to give him the right words or the strength to admit he'd screwed up. "I was upset that you were a doctor."

Most family members—or at least parents—liked the idea of their kids either becoming or dating professionals, especially doctors. So he asked, "Why would that bother you?"

"Because I was afraid you would make me look even worse in her eyes. And maybe even in my own."

Jeremy tossed the man a smile. "I'm thinking pretty highly of you right now, Max. It's not easy owning up to your mistakes."

"Thanks for not holding that against me. And for the record, it's fine with me if you're dating my sister."

"I appreciate that." It was going to be a whole lot easier for all of them if Max gave them his seal of approval.

Of course, Jeremy wasn't so sure what their relationship was or where it was going.

All he knew was that he was really looking forward to this evening—and that what he had planned for this particular date was going to be one for the record books.

Chapter Seven

When Kirsten arrived home from the grocery store and spotted Jeremy's car parked in front of her house, she quickly pulled into the driveway and reached for the reusable grocery totes that contained the formula and diapers.

Max had forgotten to pick up the baby necessities earlier, but since Anthony had been fussy and had just dozed off in Max's arms, Kirsten offered to make a quick run to the market.

She'd thought that she could get to the store and back with plenty of time to spare, but there'd been an unexpected detour on Lone Star Parkway that took her a mile out of her way in bumper-to-bumper traffic. And when she'd finally picked up the items she'd needed, as luck would have it, there was only one check-out lane open.

Fortunately, she was ready for their date. Jeremy had told her to dress warmly, so she only needed to grab a sweater.

Trouble was, she didn't like the idea that Max had been the one to greet and chat with Jeremy until she got home, finding it more than a little worrisome.

Max had been a lot mellower after she'd given him a piece of her mind and had gone shopping yesterday. But that didn't necessarily mean anything. He clearly had taken issue with Jeremy, although Kirsten couldn't imagine why.

So who knew what her brother might have said to him while they were alone?

After locking the car, she let herself into the house and found Jeremy and Max seated on the sofa. A lazy grin stretched across Jeremy's face, and one arm was resting along the back of the cushions, as though he was comfortable and at ease.

He was also wearing a pair of jeans and a sweatshirt—had he forgotten they had a date tonight?

She supposed it didn't matter. After all, he was here, wasn't he?

"I'm sorry I'm late," she said. "But everyone in Red Rock seemed to be at the market this evening, and I had to wait in line for a long time."

"Don't worry about it," Jeremy said, as he got to his feet and took the grocery bags from her. "It gave your brother and me a chance to get to know each other a little better."

"That's good." Kirsten's gaze bounced from Jeremy's smiling face to her brother's.

Ever since she'd gotten home from that shopping trip yesterday, Max had been pretty solemn and pensive. But at least he hadn't been disagreeable and snappish, which had become his habit.

She wasn't sure if Jeremy had anything to do with Max's upbeat mood or if putting her foot down and setting some boundaries had done the trick. Either way, she would count herself lucky.

"I'll put this stuff away for you," Jeremy said.

"No, let me get that." Max sprang to his feet and took the bags, then went to the kitchen, leaving Kirsten and Jeremy facing each other.

She couldn't help taking a good, hard look at him and coming to the star-struck conclusion that he was drop-dead gorgeous no matter what he wore—a lab coat, slacks and a sports jacket...

Or jeans and a sweatshirt.

She glanced down at the new black pants and the pink blouse she'd purchased yesterday. Was she overdressed?

When she glanced back up and caught his gaze, she asked "Should I change my clothes?"

"I suppose I should have said 'casual' when I said to wear something warm. You look great, but you might be more comfortable in a pair of jeans—if you have them."

She had no idea where he planned to take her—only that it was a surprise. But what the heck. She was a good sport and looked forward to spending time with him, no matter what he had in mind. "Sure. Will you give me a minute?"

"Take as long as you need."

She started toward her bedroom, then stopped and glanced over her shoulder. "Are you going to tell me where we're going? Or do I have to wait until we get there?"

"I may as well tell you now." Jeremy tossed her a crooked grin. "There's a new ice rink in town, and I thought it might be fun to give it a whirl."

Ice skating?

She wouldn't have thought that he would take her to a place like that in a million years, although, if truth be told, she would have gone with him anywhere, even if it was to the Laundromat to watch other people's clothes go round and round in a dryer.

And it *did* sound like fun.

She tossed him a schoolgirl grin. "I'll be back in a flash."

As she dashed to her room, she planned to throw a sweater on over her blouse, slip into a comfy pair of jeans, grab a thick pair of socks, brush her hair and add a bit of lipstick. But she wouldn't take long.

She was seeing a side to the doctor she hadn't expected to see—an exciting side of the man that turned her heart on end.

And she couldn't wait to get their date under way.

* * *

They arrived at the rink a little past seven that evening, and after renting skates, they started out on the ice.

Kirsten had had a pair of in-line skates as a kid and knew the basics. She'd also gone to the ice rink in San Antonio when she was a teenager, so she wasn't a novice. But she'd forgotten how difficult it was to balance.

After an hour or so, it seemed to be coming back to her. She was moving faster and feeling less apprehensive about falling.

As she zipped around the rink, she found herself smiling and laughing like a kid again.

What surprised her was how good Jeremy was. For the most part, he skated along beside her, but every once in a while, he'd take off and get a little tricky on the ice, going so far as to skate backward.

As he came up beside her again, she asked, "Where did you learn how to do that?"

"When I was in high school, I dated a girl who was a figure skater."

She wasn't sure why that surprised her. There had to be a lot of things about Jeremy that she didn't know. A lot she'd like to know.

"Her parents had wanted her to compete and maybe go to the winter Olympics," he added, "and while she wasn't as enthusiastic about the idea as they were, we used to hang out at the rink a lot."

"What happened?" she asked. "How did you two split up?"

"We went off to different colleges and drifted apart. I heard that she married a guy who later became a deputy district attorney in the Los Angeles area, and I went on to medical school."

Kirsten wondered about his other dates, the other women he'd kissed, the ones he'd made love with. But it wasn't her place to ask. And even if it was, she wasn't sure she wanted to know those kinds of details. She'd rather think that their relationship was a first of its kind for both of them.

It certainly held that kind of magic for her.

The lively music that had been playing in the background came to an end, and one of the rink employees used the speaker system to announce, "Clear the floor. It's time for couples only."

Kirsten slowed and reached for the side rail, planning to leave the ice.

"We don't need to go," Jeremy said, as he spun around to face her and reached out to her. "Come on. Let's show these kids how it's done."

Her heart clamored in her chest, urging her on, as she took hold of his hand. "I'm not sure about this. I'm doing okay as long as I stick close to the railing and go slow and easy."

"Don't be afraid." The timbre of his voice, the confidence in his tone, the way his gaze latched on to hers, reached deep into the heart of her, bolstering her confidence. And in the blink of an eye, she realized that she wouldn't be afraid to face anything, as long as he was by her side.

As the rink slowly cleared of those skating solo, leaving only the ones who'd paired up, the lights lowered. Multicolored bulbs kicked on in the corners, and a love song began to play, casting a romantic aura over the ice.

Kirsten thought they would go hand in hand around the rink, like some of the other skaters, but apparently, Jeremy had other ideas, as he took her in his arms.

"Hold on to me," he said, "And follow my lead."

Right this moment, she couldn't imagine being anywhere else than in his arms, zipping along on the ice and gazing in his eyes.

He made it all sound so easy—the skate dancing, being together. Leaning on each other.

And God only knew how badly she wanted it to be easy. But she wanted more than that, too. She wanted what she'd found in his arms, in his gaze, in his presence, to last.

Was she getting in too deep?

Or was Jeremy feeling the same way?

As he skated around the ice with Kirsten, Jeremy felt like a kid again—happy and carefree.

He hadn't done anything like this since he'd been in high school, and he hadn't realized just what he was missing.

Or was being with Kirsten what had made this evening so special? Was she the part that he'd been missing?

It was beginning to feel that way.

When the couples-only song was over and the lights

went on, Jeremy continued to skate dance with Kirsten until the rink grew too crowded to maneuver easily.

So he took her near the railing, where she felt more comfortable, and brought her to a slow stop. "Do you want to stay longer? Or would you like to get a bite to eat?"

"It's been a lot of fun, but to be honest, my ankles are getting a little wobbly and sore."

"Then let's go." He escorted her off the ice, then took her to a quiet spot where they could remove their skates and put on their street shoes.

"Do you like Mexican food?" he asked.

"Yes, why?"

"Because tacos sound really good to me. So let's stop by Red. They're hands-down the best restaurant in town."

"Then Red it is."

Twenty minutes later, Marcos Mendoza was welcoming them and reaching for menus.

"It's good to see you back," he said, as his gaze traveled from Jeremy to his date.

It was easy to see that Marcos was connecting the dots, but he was discreet enough to keep his thoughts to himself. Still, when he escorted them to a quiet little alcove with a table set for two, it was clear that he'd picked up on the romantic vibes.

Jeremy tossed him a smile, letting the younger man know that he'd read things right.

Moments later, a busboy stopped by and gave them

water, a basket of warm chips and a bowl of fresh salsa.

When they were left alone, Kirsten said, "You know, it was sure nice to come home this evening and find you and Max chatting. It seemed that you two had hit it off, and I'm glad. I haven't seen him so relaxed and happy in a long time."

Jeremy told her why that might be, going on to mention the job at the Double Crown and the plan for him to go back to school.

"No wonder he was in a good mood." Her eyes glimmered with unshed tears. "I can't thank you enough for doing that for him. He hasn't had anyone take him under their wing like that in ages."

"We'll see if he can follow through on the bargain." Jeremy reached for a chip and dipped it into the salsa. "Maybe he'll surprise us both."

Kirsten brightened. "I'm so glad to hear you say that. I've been clinging to the belief that he's a fully capable person on the inside. So it's nice to know that someone else sees it, too."

Jeremy hadn't actually *seen* anything—yet. He just hoped that Max would be able to hold a job on the Double Crown. And that he would register for continuing education classes and complete them. But Jeremy was a realist. And there were no guarantees. The kid had clearly been floundering for some time.

In all honesty, Jeremy had gone to bat for him on pure faith—but not in Max. He was doing it for Kirsten.

And since he liked seeing a smile light her face and basking in her happiness, he decided to let her assumptions and any doubts he might have slip by the wayside, opting to focus on the possibility that Max would turn over a new leaf and make them both proud.

"I don't know how to thank you for what you did," she said.

"There's no need to do that. Maybe all he needed was a lucky break and a little advice."

"I'm sure you're right." She reached for a chip and took a bite. "What kind of advice did you give him?"

"I told him that we're all on paths leading somewhere. Some of us are destined for success, others are going nowhere. Some are even headed for ruin. But there's only one person who can change the direction he's heading. And the longer he waits to do that, the tougher it'll be in the long run."

"What did he say to that?"

"He just thought about it. Hopefully, he'll realize the truth in what I told him and take the new path he's got in front of him."

Jeremy certainly hoped he would. It wasn't very often that he went to bat for someone who wasn't a tight friend or a close family member. And he could end up with egg on his face if Max blew the chance he'd been offered.

But the younger man's gratitude had seemed sincere earlier this evening. And he'd promised to give adult school and the job on the Double Crown his best shot.

Jeremy supposed time would tell.

Jeremy's surprise had turned out to be a fun, special and memorable evening. And Kirsten was sorry to see it end.

As he pulled along the curb and parked in front of her house, she wanted to invite him in for a nightcap or... whatever.

But with Max and the baby inside... Well, she was afraid that too much reality might put a damper on an otherwise dream date.

In spite of Max's earlier mood, she knew that it could all change in a heartbeat, and she didn't want to risk it. So she opted to tell Jeremy good-night at the front door.

"I had a good time," she told him.

"Me, too."

As he lowered his mouth to hers, the anticipation was almost overwhelming. Her heart opened up like a spinning kaleidoscope as she slipped her arms around his neck and lifted her lips to his.

As the kiss deepened, their breaths mingled and their tongues mated. She closed her eyes, lost in a colorful swirl of hormones, pheromones and musk.

Yet there was something else going on inside of her, something that was more than a physical reaction to an arousing kiss. And while her mind insisted it was happening too soon, that she barely knew Jeremy Fortune, it didn't seem to matter.

He was a dedicated physician who donated time to the clinic and to people who were in need. And he'd gone above and beyond for Max, something he didn't have to do.

So what else was there to know about him?

Jeremy Fortune was one in a million, and Kirsten couldn't help what she was feeling. She was falling in love with him. She didn't know if she should thank her lucky stars—or pull back and protect herself from the heartbreak. Because when he left Red Rock and returned to California, it was going to break her heart.

But she couldn't think about that now. Not when she was locked safely in his embrace, yearning for more of his touch, more of his taste.

As the kiss finally came to an end, leaving her wanting so much more than what they'd just shared, Jeremy ran his knuckles along her cheek.

"Sleep tight," he said, his voice husky.

"You, too."

Then she watched him head for his car, wishing she could call him back, that she could invite him inside and ask him to stay the night.

His stay in Red Rock is only temporary, she reminded herself. *Hold on to your heart.*

But she feared it was too late for that.

As she let herself into the house, closing the door quietly behind her, she overheard Max talking on the telephone in one of the bedrooms. She didn't usually listen in on his calls, but she couldn't help tuning into this one.

"You've got to be kidding," he said, his voice loud enough to wake the baby. "Is this a joke, Courtney? I knew something wasn't adding up."

Kirsten froze in her tracks, then slowly eased closer to the hallway that led to the bedrooms. She wished she could hear both sides of the conversation, but would settle for hearing only one.

"So I'm not listed as the father on his birth certificate?" Max asked. "Then who is?"

Kirsten hung on to each beat of the lull in conversation.

"Oh, for cripe's sake, Courtney. What do you mean you don't have his birth certificate? The hospital had to have given you one when you checked out after having him."

Kirsten wished she could hear the explanation Courtney was giving.

A surge of uneasiness rushed through her, as she realized that Max might not have legal custody of Anthony. She wondered what rights he actually had.

Could he even take the child to the doctor if he was sick? And what if Courtney wanted the baby back? Should he take a paternity test?

Max swore under his breath, then slammed the receiver down hard. Clearly, whatever Courtney had said upset him.

Kirsten waited in the living room, near the hallway. She was almost afraid to confront him, to ruin the sense of calm she'd been expecting from him when she got home tonight. But how could she not let him know what she'd overheard?

So she eased to the doorway of the bedroom, where Anthony was lying on the center of the bed. Max sat on the edge, near the telephone.

"I couldn't help overhearing a bit of your conversation with Courtney," she said. "What was that all about?"

Max blew out a sigh, then raked a hand through his hair. "Courtney's a flake."

Kirsten had gotten that vibe the first time she'd met her, but Max had been so smitten that he hadn't seen it back then. But rather than blurt out an I-told-you-so or make him feel any worse than he did right now, she tried to be respectful of him and whatever he was going through.

So she took a seat on the side of the bed, next to him. "Do you want to talk about it?"

"Not really, but I probably should." He rolled his eyes, then heaved a sigh. "When Courtney and I split up seven months ago, I didn't even know she was pregnant. Heck, I was completely shocked when she showed up with Anthony last week."

"I can understand your surprise. But I really admire you for stepping up to the plate and being such a good dad."

"That's just it," Max said. "To be honest, I'm not sure if the baby is mine or not."

"Did she just tell you that?"

"Not exactly. I had my doubts before. But how could I turn away a child that *could* be my flesh and blood?"

Kirsten saw the angst in his eyes, and her heart swelled with pride that he'd taken in the baby and was assuming responsibility, even if there was some question as to Anthony's paternity.

"We can have his DNA checked," she said.

But what would they do if the baby didn't belong to Max? Just hand him back to Courtney?

God, Kirsten couldn't do that to the poor little guy. He deserved so much better.

"Where is she?" Kirsten asked.

"I don't know. She wouldn't tell me. Apparently, she's hiding out."

That was really strange. Kirsten glanced at Anthony, who hadn't asked to be born, to be pawned off on a man who might or might not be his father. And her heart went out to him.

What would make a woman walk away from her own child? If Kirsten had a baby, she'd want him to be with her all the time.

Was Courtney really a flake, like Max had said? Or was she in some kind of serious trouble?

Kirsten bit down on her bottom lip. "Do you think we ought to try to find her? Maybe she's in trouble and needs our help."

Max chuffed. "I'd have to say that looking out for Anthony is a big help to her already."

"But you don't have legal custody." Kirsten tucked a strand of hair behind her ear. "And that could be a problem."

"I don't know," Max said. "I need some time to think about what to do."

Kirsten might have pushed or prodded him in the past, but she was learning to respect him, to let him make those calls from here on out.

As Anthony began to cry, Kirsten turned to him and picked him up. "What's the matter, sweetheart?"

"He's hungry," Max said. "I'll get his bottle."

Kirsten held the baby close and kissed his head, her lips skimming his downy soft hair. A maternal feeling fluttered over her, and she wasn't sure if she should be happy or sad.

What if she bonded with Anthony, only to learn that Max wasn't his father? What if she had to hand him back to Courtney?

Her heart crunched at the thought—not so much at losing him, but being forced to hand him over to someone who might not be good to him.

"Everything is going to be okay," she whispered, hoping she could keep her promise. "You can trust me, Anthony. I won't let anything bad happen to you."

When Max returned with the bottle of formula and handed it to her, she placed the nipple into Anthony's mouth, then watched the baby greedily latch on as if he were starving.

"Was he good for you?" she asked her brother.

"Yeah. He and I watched a little TV. The last two nights he didn't wake up until four, so I decided to keep him up tonight. I thought he might sleep until morning."

"That might work. I guess we'll have to see what happens." As Kirsten fed the baby, she studied his sweet little face. He was precious, whether he was Max's baby or not. And he really deserved a better mom than Courtney.

She looked at the phone, wondering if she ought to call Jeremy and ask his advice. He was so wise, so level-headed. He would know just what to do, what steps they ought to take.

But she couldn't dump this on him. He didn't need to deal with all the Courtney drama.

Is that what you're really worried about? an inner voice asked, forcing her to face the ugly truth. *You're not trying to protect Jeremy, you're trying to protect yourself and the whisper of a dream that might come true.*

A momentary rush of guilt swept over her as she realized that was just what she was doing.

She might have come to the conclusion that she was falling for him, but ever since meeting him in the parking lot of the clinic, she'd told herself that a relationship with her was just a passing fancy to him. That it wouldn't last, that he'd return to California and not look back. But she wasn't so sure about that anymore.

After all, he'd gone above and beyond to help her brother, getting him a job on the family-owned ranch.

That had to mean something.

He had to be seeing the possibility of a future with her. She'd felt it in the heat of his touch, seen it in the intensity in his gaze.

And if that were the case, she wasn't about to do anything that might mar the beauty of what they were feeling or destroy the dream that had taken root in her heart.

Sure, all the stars would need to align first. And she would have to pray that her luck held out. But she couldn't still the rising hope that one day she would become... Jeremy Fortune's wife.

Chapter Eight

On Saturday morning, Jeremy drove to Kirsten's house to pick up Max and take him to the Double Crown. He wanted to personally introduce Kirsten's brother to both Lily and Ruben.

He also looked forward to spending some time on the ranch hanging out with the hands, something he hadn't done since he'd been in high school.

After parking his car at the curb, he walked up the steps to the porch. But before he could lift his hand to ring the bell, Max swung open the door, boasting a Texas-size grin.

"I really appreciate you taking me out to the Double Crown," he said.

"No problem."

Max, who was dressed in a black T-shirt, worn jeans

and a pair of scuffed boots, held an old Stetson in his hands. He was clearly ready to go, but Jeremy didn't want to take off without getting a chance to talk to Kirsten.

Before he could ask to see her, she slipped up behind her brother.

"Hey," she said.

"Hey," he repeated.

A buzz of attraction and a temporary lull in conversation left him feeling a little bit like a love-struck teen who'd been approached by the head cheerleader and was struggling to find his voice.

Kirsten was wearing a pair of jeans and a white blouse today. Her hair hung loose on her shoulders, and her eyes seemed especially blue. Just looking at her set his heart on end.

"Does Max need a lunch or anything?" she asked. "I made one just in case, and packed it in a cooler."

"No, he'll be fine. The Double Crown provides meals for their hands."

There was another lull, another awkward moment.

Jeremy really needed to go, to get the show on the road, but with Kirsten standing there, close enough to catch a whiff of her floral-scented shampoo, close enough to touch, his feet seemed to take root on the porch.

There was, he supposed, only one way to remedy that.

"Would you like to take a ride out to the Double Crown with us?" he asked her. "You can meet Lily while you're there."

Her eyes sparked and her smile deepened. "It sounds

like fun." Then her expression began to fade. "But I probably shouldn't barge in on her like that."

"You'd be keeping her company," Jeremy said, realizing there was a second reason to take Kirsten along. "It'll do Lily good to have someone to talk to."

Waiting for word on Jeremy's dad had taken a real toll on her. Hell, it had taken a toll on *all* of them.

"Then that settles it," Kirsten said. "If you wouldn't mind transferring Anthony's car seat from my vehicle to yours, I'll pack his diaper bag."

At that, Max chimed in. "I'll make the switch. I just need both sets of keys."

Moments later, they were all seated in Jeremy's rented sedan and heading out of town.

Max was unusually talkative, which was a pleasant surprise. His attitude had certainly made a complete one-eighty turn, and Jeremy hoped that meant he was going to work hard at proving himself to both Ruben and Lily. If he didn't, they wouldn't keep him around.

When they reached the ranch, both Kirsten and Max scanned the acres upon acres of grazing land that lined the road.

"I can't get over the size of the place," Kirsten said.

Max merely studied the expanse of property in awe.

As they reached the sandstone wall that surrounded the buildings and the living area, Jeremy gave them a little of the history.

"Ryan Fortune's father, Kingston, bought this place nearly fifty years ago. Back then, the original house was a simple adobe structure with a flat roof trimmed with rough-hewn wood and tile. It had the same sand color as the wall around it now. But over time, as Kingston's family and his holdings grew, he added on and made renovations. But he did his best to maintain its original style."

"It's beautiful," Kirsten said.

Jeremy agreed.

Max, on the other hand, seemed taken by the large barn of weathered wood that stabled horses, the corral and fenced-off areas for branding time and the outbuildings. When he noticed the three-bedroom ranch-style home in the distance, he asked, "Who lives there?"

"That's Ruben and Rosita's house." The foreman and his wife had lived on the ranch for as long as Jeremy could remember. In fact, they'd raised their family there.

After parking in the shade of one of the few trees located near the main estate, Jeremy and his passengers got out of the car.

"Lily should be in the house," Jeremy said. "I'll introduce you to her first. That way, Kirsten and the baby can hang out inside while I take Max to meet Ruben."

He led them through the arched entryway and the wrought-iron gate that opened to the courtyard, with its large purple sage plants, twining vines and bare rosebushes that would be lush and colorful again in a few short months.

"You must love staying out here," Kirsten said, clearly taken with the Double Crown.

"I do." And he was glad he could share it with her.

Maybe someday the two of them could go horseback riding. He hadn't done anything like that since he was a teenager.

Jeremy escorted his guests along the curved stone walkway to the adobe steps that led up to the antique wooden door.

He rang the bell to let Lily know they'd arrived, but he didn't wait for her or the housekeeper to answer. Instead, he let Kirsten and Max inside.

"Lily?" he called. "We're here."

"I'll be right there," she said.

Moments later, the lovely older woman swept into the foyer, her dark eyes glimmering as she graciously welcomed both Kirsten and Max to her home.

Once the formalities were over, her gaze quickly drifted to Anthony. "What a beautiful baby."

"Thank you." Kirsten smiled down at the child, yet didn't explain that he belonged to her brother. But that was okay; Jeremy had already filled in Lily on the details.

In fact, upon hearing how Max had assumed responsibility for the baby he hadn't known about and learning that he was trying to better himself by taking the GED, Lily had been impressed and agreed to hire him.

Of course, she might have agreed anyway—strictly as a favor to Jeremy.

"Can I get you some coffee and breakfast?" Lily asked.

"No, thanks," Jeremy said. "I'm sure Max is eager to get outside and meet Ruben."

Max, who held his cowboy hat in his hands, nodded. "That's right, ma'am. Besides, I ate earlier. But thank you for the offer."

"You're welcome." Lily smiled. "Then do what you have to do. I'll take Kirsten into the great room, where we can visit and play with the baby." She reached out to stroke Anthony's cheek with her index finger.

As she did so, Kirsten smiled at the bundle in her arms.

Again, Jeremy was struck with the thought of Kirsten holding his baby, but he quickly shook it off.

Slow down, he told himself. He'd hardly gotten to know her himself. Yet he couldn't deny the feelings she'd evoked in him, unfamiliar yet warm and blood-stirring feelings he had to admit that he liked.

"I love babies," Lily said, reminding Jeremy that bringing Kirsten and Anthony along had been a good idea. Having visitors was sure to help her keep her mind off her worries—at least for today. And he couldn't help feeling a rush of pride, knowing that he'd pulled something like that together.

Of course, it was too soon to know for sure if everything would fall into place, but it appeared that his efforts just might end up being a win-win for everyone involved.

He sure hoped so. In a way, he'd stuck his neck out for Max. And he'd hate to think he'd made a mistake by bringing him to the ranch and asking Lily and Ruben to take a chance on hiring a stranger.

So far, so good, though. Max had been polite and

appreciative. He'd also shown signs of having a work ethic, although whether he'd follow through on it was still left to be seen.

Jeremy bumped Max's arm with his and nodded toward the door. "Come on. Let's go find Ruben."

Then he took Max out into the yard, leaving the women alone.

After the men headed outside, Lily turned to Kirsten and smiled. "Would you like to join me in the kitchen for a cup of tea and some blueberry muffins?"

"That sounds nice." Kirsten tightened her grip on the handle of Anthony's carrier and followed Lily through the great room, which was dominated by a large open hearth on one wall.

She slowed her pace and noted the curved, wooden-framed glass doors that opened up to a lovely courtyard. Even in February, the plants out there were lush. She wondered what it would look like during spring and summer, with the flowers blooming.

As she followed her hostess to the kitchen, their shoes clicked upon the tile floors, where hand-woven rugs in Native American and Mexican patterns had been carefully placed.

The farther Kirsten went into the house, with its mixture of both modern and antique furnishings, the more impressed she was with the decor.

When they entered the large functional kitchen with all the modern conveniences, Kirsten noticed that it still reflected the same Southwestern influence as the rest of the house and couldn't help sharing her impressions. "Your home is beautiful, Lily. You must love living here."

"Thank you. I do. In fact, I can't imagine living anywhere else."

Kirsten understood the feeling. At one time, she hadn't been able to imagine living in any other house but the one she'd purchased on her own and decorated to suit her. Yet the longer she knew Jeremy, the more she was thinking about California.

Would she like it there?

Oh, for Pete's sake, she scolded herself. How could she allow a question like that to even form in her mind? At this point, she had no reason to believe Jeremy would even invite her to go with him to California. And even though she sensed their relationship was becoming stronger each day and that they were growing closer, she didn't want to make any unwarranted assumptions until he gave her reason to do so.

As Lily poured water in a teapot and put it on to boil, she asked, "So how long have you and Jeremy been dating?"

"Actually, we've only formally gone out a couple times. But we've been seeing each other a lot."

"I thought that you might be." Lily smiled. "I haven't seen much of him lately."

"I'm sorry." Kirsten knew that Lily was just as worried about Jeremy's father as he was—maybe more so. And that was why he'd been staying with her and offering his support.

"Please don't be sorry about him being away from the ranch," Lily said. "I'm a romantic at heart and can appreciate it when two people are attracted to each other. Besides, it's time for Jeremy to loosen up and have some fun. He's been so focused on his medical practice over the years that I was afraid he would let life pass him by."

"It's been fun for me, too. Meeting Jeremy has been a real blessing." Not only was he a perfect gentleman and one of the nicest guys in the entire world, he'd also taken Max under his wing. And Kirsten would always appreciate that—no matter what direction their relationship took.

"I felt the same way you do when my friendship with William took a romantic turn," Lily said. "We were going to get married on New Year's Day." Her eyes grew wistful and misty, and the tone of her voice softened. "But he didn't make it to the ceremony."

Kirsten's heart went out to the older woman. "I can't imagine how terrible that must have been for you. How terrible it still must be."

"At first, people suspected that he'd gotten cold feet and took off to avoid marrying me, but I knew better than that. He was looking forward to the wedding as much or more than I was." Lily took two teacups and saucers from the cupboard, placing one in front of Kirsten and the other for herself. "Then three days after his disappearance, his wrecked vehicle was found. He'd been involved in an accident. Or rather, his Mercedes was."

Jeremy had mentioned that to Kirsten. And the fact that there hadn't been any sign of William.

"We wondered if he'd been kidnapped, which could be the case," Lily added, as she pulled several choices of tea from the pantry. "But we never received a call or a ransom note."

Kirsten couldn't help thinking that there'd been some other kind of foul play, yet what?

And why?

As the kettle began to whistle, Lily removed it from the stove and poured water into each cup. "I can't explain it, but I have a very strong feeling that William will return. That he'll be all right. And that we'll be able to marry one day."

"I can understand you wanting to hold on to hope," Kirsten said.

"It's more than that." Lily returned the kettle to the stove. "You may not believe this, but I can almost hear a voice whispering to me and telling me to hang in there, that he'll be home soon. That everything will be okay again." Lily gave a little shrug. "I'm sure that sounds odd to you."

"No, it doesn't." Kirsten knew how difficult William's disappearance had been on Jeremy, and she suspected the other brothers felt the same way. But it had to be especially difficult for Lily, who'd lost Ryan to death and then found love again with William.

How sad to be alone once more. She hoped the family would get news soon—one way or the other. Yet in spite of her best wishes for a happy resolution, a realization shuddered through her.

If and when William was found, Jeremy would no longer have a reason to stay in Red Rock.

The hours seemed to fly by as Kirsten and Lily spent the day together. In spite of their age difference, they really hit it off.

Maybe that was because Kirsten had missed having a mother figure in her life. Or maybe that was only part of it, since she truly liked Lily Fortune as a person.

They'd had a light lunch of lentil soup and homemade French bread, which was unbelievably delicious.

When Jeremy and Max came back into the house in the late afternoon, grinning from ear to ear and clearly having enjoyed their time outdoors, Lily insisted that they stay for dinner, as well.

"It's up to Kirsten," Jeremy said. "I'm game if she is."

Feeling as if she'd somehow become a part of the Fortune family and basking in the acceptance, Kirsten had agreed.

So they'd had an early dinner of grilled chicken with a red sauce, Spanish rice and a zucchini and corn dish that Kirsten thought was especially tasty.

To top it off, Lily had brought out a lemon pound cake and servings of mango sherbet.

All in all, it had been a lovely day. And now they were saying their goodbyes.

"It's been nice having company," Lily said, as she

walked them out to Jeremy's car. "I'm afraid that, since William's disappearance... Well, as much as I believe that he'll come back to me, it's not always easy to stay positive. And having company today helped."

"I had a great time," Kirsten told the older woman, as Max took the baby from her to secure him in his car seat.

Jeremy gave Lily a hug. "Thanks for being such a great hostess—as always. I'll be back after I take Kirsten and Max home."

Moments later, they were on their way to Kirsten's house. As the car sped along the highway that would take them to nearby Red Rock, Max couldn't seem to thank Jeremy enough for the day he'd spent on the ranch. Every sentence seemed to start with "Ruben said..."

"I'm glad you're going to like working there," Jeremy said.

"I love that kind of work. I can't wait to start."

They rode along in silence for a while, then Max said, "Thanks for hanging out all day with me. I know you had other things you could have done."

"Actually, it gave me an opportunity to relive all the summers my brothers and I used to stay on the ranch with Lily and Ryan. I probably had a better day than you had."

"I doubt it," Max said.

Kirsten couldn't help smiling at her brother's good fortune. The job was sure to be a godsend for both her and Max, yet she kept quiet, listening to the men talk.

After all, the trip out to the Double Crown had

been for Max's benefit; Kirsten had only gone along for the ride.

But what a ride it had been.

She settled back in her seat, her heart overflowing with warmth and pride. The day had unfolded nicely, leaving her pleased, content and…happy.

Her brother had a job he was excited about. And he was going to register for classes at the adult school on Monday morning, then drive out to the ranch to work for the rest of the day. She'd never seen him so enthusiastic about the future. In fact, he seemed like a whole new person.

And Kirsten had Jeremy to thank for that.

Her life, it seemed, had changed dramatically since meeting him—and in a wonderful way. Just his smile, his woodsy scent and his touch could set a thrill rushing through her.

She wasn't sure what to make of their romance, but she knew that she wanted it to grow into all that it could be.

The trip home was over before she knew it, and she found herself wishing the night would go on and on.

If Max and the baby weren't staying with her, she would have invited Jeremy in for a nightcap…and a whole lot more. But when the two of them made love, she wanted the mood and the atmosphere to be special, to be perfect.

So she'd have to settle for a good-night kiss. Though *settle* was hardly the right word, since Jeremy's kisses weakened her knees and turned her inside out.

After Jeremy parked the car at the curb, Max got out and removed Anthony from the car seat.

"Kirsten," he said, "if you don't mind holding the baby for me, I'll switch his seat back to your car."

"All right." She took Anthony in her arms, glad to help. Yet she hoped Max would take the baby inside when he was finished and give them some alone time. She was eager for an opportunity to kiss Jeremy goodnight. Maybe she'd even get an answer to the where-do-we-go-from-here question she'd been afraid to ask.

Fortunately, she didn't have to wait long. The seat had been transferred in no time at all. Then Max took Anthony into the house, leaving her and Jeremy outside.

As they lingered in the front yard, where the porch light cast a golden glow on them, she was again tempted to ask Jeremy to come inside—and to stay the night. But with Max in the house... Well, it just didn't feel right.

"Thanks for riding out to the ranch with us," Jeremy said.

"I had a wonderful time. Lily is one of the nicest people I've ever met. She's a great decorator, hostess and cook."

"I'm glad you liked her. She's always been special to me."

They stood like that for a moment, caught up in the silence and the buzz of pheromones.

"I'd invite you in," she said. "But..."

"I understand."

"You do?"

"It's a little crowded in your house tonight."

She wondered if he was as disappointed about that as she was.

"So how about dinner tomorrow night?" he asked. "I've got to attend a board meeting for the Fortune Foundation on behalf of the medical center on Monday, which is Valentine's Day. But we can celebrate on Sunday instead."

Celebrate? The day set aside for lovers?

That certainly sounded as though their relationship was progressing. And that her instincts had been right.

"It sounds great," she said.

"I'm glad to hear it." He cupped her face and brushed his thumbs across her cheeks.

Their gazes met and locked. Passion simmered in his eyes, and her heart raced. The anticipation alone made her rethink her decision not to invite him in the house, no matter who was inside.

Had that been a mistake? One she ought to remedy?

She wanted so very badly to drag him into her bedroom, lock the door and turn up the radio so that anything they said and did would be their secret to keep. But she wanted so much more than that for their first time.

As his mouth lowered to hers, she closed her eyes and parted her lips. Her arms looped around his neck, and she slipped into his embrace.

He kissed her deeply, thoroughly. And as their tongues mated, as their breaths mingled, she held him tight, wanting him. Wanting more.

His hands slid along the curve of her hips, resting on her derriere and staking an intimate claim. So she leaned forward and rubbed her hips against his, making a claim of her own.

She wasn't sure how long the kiss lasted—long enough to make it difficult to stand without holding on. Long enough to stir an empty ache in the most feminine part of her.

Her only complaint was that it ended before she was ready to let go.

But then again, she wasn't sure if she would ever be ready to pull away from Jeremy.

"Maybe we ought to have dinner at one of the nicer hotels in town," he said. "We'd have the option of getting a room, which might make things a whole lot easier."

A boyish grin implied that he was teasing, yet desire had darkened the blue of his eyes, which made her wonder if he was testing her response.

"I'll wear my favorite dress," she said. "And I'll go wherever you want to take me."

There. She'd said it. And she'd been telling the truth. She wanted to go wherever their kisses took them, because that last one had whispered of forever.

"I'll talk to you tomorrow," he said.

She nodded, even though tomorrow seemed like a very long time from now. Then she stood alone on the porch and watched him turn and stride toward his car. She struggled with the urge to call him back and to ask him about the future. Instead, she bit her tongue. She would just have to bide her time until he brought up the subject.

But that didn't keep the questions from bombarding her like buckshot.

Would Jeremy ask her to leave town and join him in California?

If so, would she go?

As much as she'd like to remain living in her house in Red Rock—with him—she realized that wasn't likely.

Jeremy had a successful medical practice in Sacramento. And being away from his colleagues and his patients had to be tough on him.

Of course he did have family here. And he'd taken a leave of absence and had no immediate plans to return to California—as far as she knew. He'd also started working at the clinic and seemed to like it.

Would he decide to stay in Red Rock?

He might. But *then* what?

Would he and Kirsten remain lovers? Or would they marry and start a family?

The questions were legion. And she both longed for and feared the answers.

Chapter Nine

After Jeremy drove away, Kirsten went into the house and softly closed the door. She could hear Max talking to someone down the hall, and while she couldn't make out his words, she also felt his upbeat tone.

Had he actually chuckled? She hoped so. He'd been miserable for way too long, and it was good to see him happy for a change.

She walked past his closed door, then entered her own room. After shutting herself inside, she blew out a sigh. What a day this had been.

And *oh,* she sighed, what a man.

A grin splashed across her face as she realized that Max wasn't the only one in the house who was happy.

While undressing in her private bathroom, she relived that amazing kiss she and Jeremy had just shared, a kiss that had been more of a kickoff to foreplay than a way in which to end the day.

As she climbed into the shower and let the warm water sluice over her, thoughts of Jeremy sent her imagination soaring.

Soft music and candlelight.

Heated kisses.

Blood-stirring caresses.

Clothing falling by the wayside, bodies tumbling onto the bed in a fevered rush.

Making love all night long.

By the time she'd finished showering, she was sorry she'd let him go back to the ranch.

But she had, so she was stuck sleeping alone and dreaming of what might have been.

After putting on her most comfortable flannel nightgown, she turned down the covers and climbed into bed. The sheets were freshly laundered, the house was quiet and her heart was strumming with contentment. Still, it took forever to fall asleep. Her mind was too caught up thinking about what tomorrow night might bring.

She couldn't help wishing that he *would* take her to a hotel and that they'd end their date by making love.

Should she pack an overnight bag just in case? Should she tell Max that he'd be handling the baby care duties on his own since she might not come home at all?

Oh, good grief. Jeremy had been smiling when he implied that they could check into a room.

She'd sure be embarrassed if she walked out with her

makeup bag and toothbrush, only to find that Jeremy *had* been joking about the hotel.

Squeezing her eyes tight, she did her best to shut out the thoughts and try to sleep. But each time she started to drift off, she would imagine them in nearby San Antonio, walking hand in hand along the River Walk at midnight. Or slow dancing at a trendy downtown jazz club to the sensual sounds made by a guy playing the sax.

She wasn't sure what time it was when she finally fell asleep, but it was well after midnight. She slept well, but certainly not long enough.

Just before seven, she woke to the hearty aroma of fresh coffee brewing. Deciding she could use a little caffeine, she threw off the covers and wrapped herself in a robe. Then she went into the kitchen, where Max was standing near the toaster, waiting for his bread to pop out.

He was smiling to himself, and she suspected it had something to do with his new job.

"It's nice to see you in a good mood," she said, as she reached for a cup and poured herself some coffee.

"I can't believe it myself. Just last week, I felt like a loser. I didn't think I'd ever climb out of the rut I was in. But with a couple good breaks, it seems like things are finally turning around."

"You mean the new job at the Double Crown?"

"That, too. But I just got a call from Kelly Thompson last night, after I took Anthony into the house and put him to bed. And we talked for hours."

Kirsten hadn't heard the name before. "Who's Kelly?"

"She's a girl I met while I worked at the feed store. You'd really like her. She's a lot like you."

In what way? Kirsten wondered.

Instead, she asked, "How long have you two been dating?"

"Well, that's just it. We went out for a couple months, but then I was laid off and couldn't afford to take her out anymore, which really sucked. I was so embarrassed about being unemployed, that I just backed off and quit calling her. Know what I mean?"

Kirsten nodded. That was what Max always did with her, too. He just withdrew.

"But seeing you and Jeremy coming together made me realize how much I missed having someone in my life, too. So I called Kelly on Friday and left a message on her answering machine."

"And she called you back last night?"

"Yeah. Apparently, she wasn't going to at first. But then she gave in. We talked for a long time, and I leveled with her. She seemed to understand, so I asked her out to dinner. But I told her I was waiting on a paycheck, so it wouldn't be a fancy place."

"I'm sure she was okay with that."

"She was better than okay. She told me not to worry about anything. She had a new recipe she wanted to try out, and that I should go to her house for dinner instead."

"That's great."

"I think so, too."

"Did you tell her about Anthony?"

Max's smile drooped. "No, not yet. I... Well, before I do that, I'd like to see how things go tonight."

Kirsten could understand that. She still found herself tiptoeing around Jeremy, too.

"Anthony is precious," she told her brother. "And if Kelly's the kind of woman you think she is, a baby won't scare her off."

"I'm sure you're right. But having Anthony in my life also means that Kelly might end up having to deal with Courtney, too. And I hate to have that dumped on her."

Kirsten had the same apprehension about letting Jeremy in on too much of that kind of drama. "Maybe we'll both luck out, and Courtney will be history."

"I sure hope so. But she's kind of like a bad penny and keeps calling or showing up when I least expect it."

"Just take it slow and easy," Kirsten said.

"That's what I plan to do."

When the toast popped up, her brother turned around and reached for the butter.

Kirsten took a sip of her coffee. She sure hoped Max's romance worked out for him, just as it seemed to be doing for her and Jeremy.

But speaking of romance, she really ought to tell Max that she had plans tonight, that she wouldn't be able to watch Anthony for him, but she couldn't bring herself to do it.

For the longest time, she'd feared her brother would

never be happy again. That he'd do something stupid and get into trouble. That he'd be a failure.

Having a nice girl in his life might make all the difference in the world. So how could Kirsten not look after Anthony for him?

She would just have to sacrifice her plans for his— which was what she usually ended up doing.

But wasn't that what love was all about?

Moments later, the telephone rang. She answered and found Jeremy on the line.

"What are you up to?" he asked.

"Just having coffee. Why?"

"No reason. I just called to say good morning."

How sweet, she thought. The only thing nicer would have been to wake up in his arms and hear him say it to her.

"I also wanted to tell you that I made dinner reservations at the San Antonio Monarch Hotel," he added. "Are you still willing to go anywhere with me?"

Boy, was she. But how did she let him know that their Valentine's Day celebration wasn't going to work out the way they wanted it to?

Come right out and tell him, she supposed. "There's nothing I'd like to do more than go with you tonight, but Max already has plans for this evening. And I've got to watch Anthony."

"Can you get a sitter?" he asked.

"I don't know who I'd ask." She blew out a sigh, realizing that she was even more disappointed than she'd thought she'd be. "But why don't you come over around four? We'll have the house to ourselves. I can fix an early dinner, then we can…"

She didn't continue, but apparently, she didn't have to.

"Sounds like a plan. I'll see you then."

An hour later, while she was holding Anthony and trying to finish making a grocery list for the dinner she had planned, the doorbell rang.

"I'll get it," she called out to Max, who was in the back of the house.

When she swung open the door, she spotted Cassie Rodriguez, the neighbor's daughter, on the porch.

"I was wondering if you'd like to buy some magazines," the teenager asked. "It's for a good cause. My church youth group is going on a mission trip to an orphanage in Mexico, so we're trying to earn money."

Kirsten smiled. "I'd be happy to buy a couple magazines, Cassie. Come on inside."

"Cool." The dark-haired teen grinned, revealing a shiny set of braces, as she entered the house and handed over the catalog. "Want me to hold the baby for you?"

"If you don't mind. Thanks." Kirsten passed the infant to the girl, then took a seat on the sofa and began thumbing through the pages. "I'd like to order *Parents* magazine. And also *Better Homes and Gardens*."

"All right," Cassie said, adding, "Your baby is really cute."

"Isn't he? His name is Anthony, and he's my nephew. If you don't mind holding him a little longer, I'll go get my checkbook."

"I don't mind at all. I love babies. In fact, I watch over my little cousins all the time."

While Kirsten went for her purse, she had a light bulb moment. The Rodriguez family was really nice. And since Cassie was experienced with kids…

As she returned to the living room, she asked, "Would you like to watch Anthony for Max and me tonight?"

"Sure. That would be great."

Wouldn't it be?

Now Kirsten could tell Max that he would have to relieve the sitter when he got home from Kelly's house. And then she would call Jeremy back and tell him that their night in San Antonio was still on.

Jeremy hoped he hadn't made any false assumptions by thinking that Kirsten wanted to spend the night with him in San Antonio, but he'd seen the agreement in her eyes. So he let Lily know that he probably wouldn't be home tonight, that there was no reason for her to worry.

When he rang the bell, Kirsten answered, looking like she'd just stepped out of a beauty ad in *Cosmopolitan* magazine wearing a simple but classic black dress and heels. Her hair had been swept into a chic twist, revealing diamond studs that sparkled in her ears. But the precious stones weren't any more dazzling than her smile.

"You look beautiful," he said.

"So do you." She flushed, then gave a little shrug. "Well, you know what I mean."

With her on his arm, he actually *felt* dashing.

"Are you ready to go?" he asked.

She seemed hesitant, then bit down on her bottom lip.

"Is something wrong?"

"No, it's just that…" She blew out a little sigh, then crossed her arms. "Should I bring anything other than a purse?"

He laughed, glad that he'd called it right, that she wasn't having second thoughts. "A toothbrush might come in handy."

"Good," she said, her eyes brightening. "I packed my makeup bag just in case. I wasn't sure if you were serious about…" She looked up at him, flushed again.

Damn, she was cute when she was off stride.

He smiled. "I guess you could say that I was covering my ass. If you wouldn't have liked the idea, I would have insisted that I'd only been teasing."

"Aren't you tricky," she said, as she went to get her bag.

Before walking out the door, Kirsten gave Cassie, the sitter, some last-minute instructions. "Max said he would be home by eleven. I hope that's not too late."

"Not at all," the girl said.

"Good. I left his cell-phone number on the kitchen counter. He said to tell you to give him a call if you had any problems."

"Okay, cool. But I'm sure everything will be fine."

"I'm sure it will be." Kirsten thanked her again, and then they left.

"I'm glad you found a babysitter," Jeremy said, as they headed for his car.

"So am I. In fact, when I told Max that I'd lined up Cassie to watch Anthony this evening, he was relieved to know we had some child-care options from now on."

An hour later, they'd checked into their suite at the Monarch, a new hotel overlooking the San Antonio River Walk.

Kirsten held her breath when she opened the glass sliding door and stepped out onto the balcony. "Look at this view."

He was looking. But it wasn't the San Antonio sights that were impressing him. It was the stunning beauty who had kicked off her heels at the door and had crossed the room in her bare feet.

She turned, and with her back to the city, faced him and blessed him with a stunning smile. "I've never been in a room like this."

He'd never been *anywhere* with a woman like her. And while he'd planned to take her to eat at the five-star restaurant on the top floor of the hotel, he wouldn't mind having room service and enjoying the privacy of their room.

"Do you want to go to dinner?" he asked. "Or, if you like the view, we can order in."

"Honestly? I don't mind eating in. It might be nice."

"I think so, too."

After looking over the room service menu, Jeremy ordered a bottle of his favorite Napa Valley merlot and the chateaubriand for two. Then he turned on some soft music on the CD player and joined Kirsten on the balcony.

As he slid up behind her, he caught the whiff of her shampoo—something with an appealing fragrance. "I like the scent of whatever you're wearing. What is it?"

She turned to him and smiled. "It's called Lilac Garden."

As her gaze zeroed in on his, he suddenly wanted to take her in his arms, to kiss her senseless. But what was the rush?

It might be best to get dinner out of the way first, although he was no longer hungry.

Not for food, anyway.

In the background, Michael Bublé sang "Baby, you've got what it takes." And Jeremy had to admit, that when it came to Kirsten, the lyrics were spot-on.

He ran the knuckles of one hand along her cheek, amazed at the softness of her skin.

As his hormones rushed and his pulse rate spiked, he had half a notion to scoop her up in his arms and carry her to the bed, but he wasn't going to rush it. They had all night long.

He took hold of her hand. "Dance with me."

Her eyes glimmered as he led her back into the room and took her in his arms. As they swayed to the music, as their hearts beat as one, Jeremy wondered if he'd ever want to make love to a woman more than he did with this one.

When the music ended, he kissed her—slow and seductively. He took his time, exploring her mouth with his tongue, and her body with his hands. As she leaned into him, as her hands ran along his back to his butt and up again, he wanted to feel the length of her against him—skin to skin.

But with dinner coming, he wouldn't risk it. When they made love, he didn't want any interruptions.

Moments later—or maybe it had been an hour, since time seemed to be standing still when he was with her—a knock sounded at the door.

"Room service," he said.

"Are you hungry?" she asked.

"Only for you." The truth of that hung in the pheromone-charged air as he let the bellman in and tipped him for his service.

Minutes later, they were alone again.

A small, linen-draped table, which had been adorned with a single red rose and a sprig of baby's breath, had been set up on the balcony, providing a romantic ambiance, complete with a view of the city.

It was a bit chilly tonight, Jeremy thought, as he lifted the bottle of merlot and filled their glasses. Then, he raised his in a toast. "Happy Valentine's Day, Kirsten."

"Thank you for going out of your way to make it special." She offered him a smile. "It's definitely going to be a memorable one for me."

He hoped so, because he was going to do everything he could to make sure that it was.

He clinked his glass against hers.

They'd barely had a sip of merlot, when he noticed Kirsten stroking the tops of her arms.

He'd been right; it *was* too cold for her.

"Here, take this." He slipped off his black sports jacket and gave it to her.

"What about you?" she asked.

"I'll be fine." In fact, kissing her earlier had shot a blast of heat through his bloodstream, so he wasn't the least bit cold.

He was, however, ready to zip through dinner and get to something a whole lot more memorable than food.

Kirsten didn't know when she'd had a nicer meal—or better company. Everything about this evening—other than the chill in the air—was perfect. But even then, bundled up in Jeremy's jacket and breathing his scent that lingered on the fabric, she had no reason to complain.

When they finished eating, Jeremy pushed the table into the bedroom area and out into the hall. Then he picked up the phone and asked someone to take it away.

Kirsten, who was still barefoot, removed his jacket and hung it in the closet.

"How about another dance?" he said, reaching out his hand to her.

She couldn't think of anything she'd like better.

Scratch that. She could think of *one* other thing, but she had a feeling that would soon follow.

As she slipped back into his embrace, the music playing softly in the background, she placed her hand on his chest, felt the steady beat of his heart.

Wrapped in Jeremy's arms, surrounded by his warmth

and his strength, she felt a security she'd never known before. And a realization she hadn't been ready for.

She was falling mindlessly in love with Jeremy, risking possible heartbreak in the future. And all she could do was hope he was feeling the same way about her.

They continued to sway to the romantic beat, dancing cheek to cheek and heart to heart, until Jeremy slowly drew them to a stop.

When Kirsten looked up and caught the intensity in his gaze, her pulse spiked with desire and an ache settled deep in her feminine core.

She wasn't a virgin, but she wasn't all that experienced in the ways of lovemaking, either. Yet something told her it didn't matter. That either way, she would never feel this way about another man again, never want one so badly.

Empowered by absolute love and pure passion, she placed her hand on Jeremy's cheek and pulled his mouth to hers.

Their lips came together as if their last kiss had never ended, as if they'd merely put it on hold. Yet this time, they kissed with a hungry desperation.

Their tongues mated, his breaths became hers, and Kirsten finally knew what it meant for two to become one.

Unable to get enough of him, she threaded her fingers through his hair and held him tight.

His hands explored her body, running the length of her torso—over, under, around. As he cupped her breast, kneading it slowly, his thumb skimmed across her nipple and she feared that she would collapse in a heated pool at his feet.

Finally, he reached for the zipper at the back of her dress. She stopped kissing him long enough to say, "Good idea," and to help him peel off the fabric.

Before long, they were both undressed, aroused and ready.

She skimmed her fingers down his muscular chest, taking time to flick his nipples to see if they were as sensitive as hers. She had her answer when he flinched, then clamped his hand over hers—holding her captive, it seemed.

"You're making me crazy," he said.

She smiled. "In a good way, I hope."

"In a *very* good way."

After throwing back the covers on the bed, he scooped her into his arms and deposited her on the mattress, where he joined her. Within a heartbeat, they'd both taken up right where they'd left off.

As he tongued the soft spot under her ear, then trailed wet kisses down her throat, her breath caught, which only seemed to urge him on.

He suckled her nipples, first one and then the other, until she feared she would cry out in need.

His kisses were magic, and so was his touch. But she'd had all the foreplay she could handle without coming apart at the seams.

"I want you inside me," she said, her breathing laden with desire. *"Now."*

He seemed only too happy to oblige, as he lifted up

and hovered over her, preparing to complete what they'd started, what they both wanted.

She opened for him, placing her hands over the curve of his buttocks, stroking and caressing while guiding him right where she wanted him, where she needed him to be.

He pushed inside her, and she arched to meet him halfway. Her body responded to his, taking and giving, as he pumped in and out. Their pleasure built, multiplying a hundredfold. And when she reached a peak so high she thought she might touch the moon and the stars, her body began to contract.

She cried out with pleasure, just as he shuddered and released, spilling into her.

For a moment, she realized they hadn't used protection—which really ought to shake her up. But for some reason, she wasn't all that concerned.

She loved Jeremy. And she'd like nothing better than to be his wife and to have his baby.

There was, however, one thing she really ought to be afraid of. And that was his return to California.

Please, she prayed silently, *don't let him leave Red Rock.*

Not unless he plans to take me with him.

Chapter Ten

Talk about passion and chemistry.

Kirsten and Jeremy had been so caught up in the heat of the moment that they'd neglected to open the box of condoms he'd brought along.

"Damn," he'd uttered, when he'd first realized what had happened. "I can't believe this. I never take risks like that."

At first, she'd been a little uneasy about his reaction, but when he asked her to forgive him for the slip-up, she relaxed, thinking he'd been concerned about her worries as much as his own.

"It's not any more your fault than mine," she'd said, counting the days in her head and trying to convince herself that it had been a safe time of the month.

Of course, that didn't always mean anything.

An unplanned pregnancy certainly would be inconvenient, she decided, but not the end of the world—to her, anyway. She wasn't sure how he'd take it, though.

They'd gone on to make love several more times that night, relishing every delicious moment, but they'd used precaution from then on.

She finally fell asleep around two, wrapped in Jeremy's arms and completely sated from their lovemaking.

Yet sometime before dawn, a baby cried.

Footsteps sounded, heavy and hurried.

Dark shadows swept over the Portacrib, cold and breezy.

Heartbeats thumped, loud enough to shake the room.

More footsteps.

Another cry.

Anthony. Someone grabbed him and ran, disappearing with him in the eerie dark shadows.

Kirsten chased after them as hard and as fast as she could, but her feet moved like tree trunks rooted deeply into the ground. She tried to scream for help, but the words only gurgled in her throat.

Oh, my God. The baby!

She shot up in bed, eyes wide, heart thumping. Her breathing was ragged, as if she'd truly been running for all she was worth.

But in a desperate attempt to make sense of it all, she scanned the darkened hotel room, listening for a cry. But she heard only the soft sounds of breathing, saw nothing other than the naked man stretched out on the bed beside her, a sheet draped over his waist.

It had only been a dream.

No, she decided. Not a dream, but a nightmare in which someone had snatched Anthony.

A cold chill ran down her spine, striking fear through every cell of her body.

Could it have been a vision from the past?

A premonition of what was to come?

An omen, maybe, that told her Anthony wouldn't be safe unless she was around to protect him?

She combed her fingers through the tangled strands of her hair. As much as she would like to wake Jeremy, to ask him to hold her until the scary thoughts subsided, until her heart stopped racing and her breathing slowed back to normal, she couldn't bring herself to do it.

Not without dragging him into all the Courtney drama. Families like the Fortunes didn't have things like that to deal with.

So she carefully slid out from under the covers, trying not to jostle the mattress and wake Jeremy. Then she climbed from bed and walked softly to the dressing area, where she'd spotted two white bathrobes earlier. Choosing one, she slipped it on, then went into the living room and took a seat on the sofa.

She wasn't sure how long she sat there, twenty minutes or so, when she heard the bedding rustle and the mattress squeak.

Jeremy was stirring.

"Kirsten?" he called out.

"I'm in here."

He got out of bed, crossed the room and joined her in the living area. The sun was just starting to rise, and as it peered through the window, she could make out her lover's naked form.

His hair was tousled, his brow furrowed.

"Are you okay?" he asked.

"I'm fine," she lied.

Something sparked in his eyes, an emotion too difficult for her to read—compassion? Worry?

"Are you having second thoughts about what we did?" he asked.

"No, it's not that."

He took a seat beside her. "Are you worried because we didn't use a condom that first time?"

She placed her hand on his knee, felt his warmth, his strength. "It was careless of us. But no, I'm not stressed about it."

"Are you sure?"

The man had good instincts and had clearly picked up on whatever vibes she was giving out.

"A pregnancy wouldn't be very convenient," she admitted. "But I think we're safe. And if not, then I'll deal with it."

He placed his hand over hers, as it rested on his knee. "But you won't deal with it alone. We're in it together."

His words and their meaning soothed something deep inside her, easing the fear she'd felt earlier.

They were a team now, it seemed. And she relished

the possibility of having someone on her side, in her corner.

And not just anyone. Jeremy Fortune was a man to be admired. And she was lucky to have met him—and to have caught his interest.

"Thanks." She'd been on her own for so long that she'd forgotten how good it felt to have someone's support. "I appreciate that."

"Is there something I can do to help?" he asked.

He clearly knew she was upset about something, and while she didn't want to tell him exactly what it was, she supposed she had to say something.

But what? She wasn't even sure what was really bothering her.

Finally she said, "Do you believe in premonitions?"

He was quiet for a moment. "I don't know. I never have in the past. But a while back, I had a dream that seemed incredibly real. And it…well, it might have been a premonition of some kind. A good one, though. Why?"

"What did you dream about?" she asked. "Do you mind telling me about it?"

He didn't respond right away, and she wondered why. Was he afraid to share it with her? Even after the intimacy they'd shared last night?

Was he holding back to protect himself, just as she was?

"Let's just say it had something to do with the future," he said. "I'm not sure what it meant, if anything, but it seems to be coming true."

Her tummy knotted, and she felt the bile rise

to her throat. So he *did* have reason to believe in premonitions.

"Did you have a dream, too?" he asked.

She nodded. "But it wasn't a good one. I'm worried about Anthony."

"Are you afraid Max won't take care of him?"

"No, it's not that. Max is really good with him."

He stroked the top of her hand. "Then what are you worried about?"

"I don't know. It's just a vibe, I guess. A bad one. And I can't explain it." She turned to him, hopeful, willing to let him convince her that everything would be okay.

Jeremy didn't like seeing Kirsten so upset. And since she'd obviously had a nightmare of some kind, he was sorry that he'd even mentioned his own dream to her, the one about the woman on the porch holding a baby.

The woman who looked a lot like Kirsten.

To be honest, he wasn't even sure if she actually resembled the dream woman or not. Maybe he'd just wanted her to. Maybe it was a matter of attraction at first sight combined with a little self-fulfilling prophecy.

Who knew for sure? But he had to admit that he'd begun to feel something for her, something he imagined love might feel like.

Either way, he wasn't quite sure what it was or what to do about it. All he knew was that he hated to see her upset, and that he would do whatever he could to make her feel better.

"I really don't believe in premonitions," he said, which

was the truth, no matter how much stock he wanted to take in the dream he'd had about her. "I'm sure you just had a run-of-the-mill nightmare. There's nothing to worry about."

She didn't respond, yet she kept her hand on his knee, clinging to him, it seemed. And he was glad he could be there for her, but he wanted her to come back to bed, where he could kiss away the goblins and bogeymen.

"Are you sure you don't want to talk about it?" he asked.

"No. I'd rather not. It's just that…well, that poor little baby is so vulnerable right now. And he doesn't have anyone but me." She combed her fingers through her hair, then realized that wasn't exactly true. "Okay. So he's got Max, too."

"It sounds to me as if you're bonding with him," Jeremy said.

She glanced up and released a wistful grin. "Yes, I guess I am. Maybe it's just some weird maternal instinct I hadn't realized I had."

If things developed between them, if they decided to have kids of their own someday, he liked knowing that she had those instincts, that she'd be a good mother.

She blew out a sigh. "I hate feeling like this. No one told me how stressful parenthood could be."

He smiled and slipped an arm around her, drawing her against him, holding her close. Then he placed a kiss on the side of her head. "I'm sure you're right. My mom used to make it look like a breeze, but raising five kids had to be tough. I know my brothers and I didn't make it easy on her."

She continued to rest against him, making him feel like some kind of a hero when he really hadn't done anything.

"There were five kids in your family?" she asked.

"Yep. All boys."

He could feel the tension ease in her shoulders, which must be proof that he was doing something right. And that was a relief. He'd been in uncharted emotional waters ever since he'd met her.

"I wish I could have been part of a large family," she said. "It was always just me, my brother and our mom."

"A big family is nice if you're willing to take the good with the bad."

"What do you mean?"

"My brothers and I didn't always get along, and we had our share of bloody noses, black eyes and broken bones. But we were—and still are—very close. I wouldn't trade them or my childhood for anything."

They sat like that for a while, caught up in their thoughts, in their memories. In the emotion their love-making had stirred within them.

Then, as the sun began to rise higher in the sky, lighting the room, he realized that they wouldn't be going back to bed anytime soon.

"How about some coffee?" he asked. "I can call room service and ask them to bring up a carafe."

"Actually, that sounds good." She sat up straight,

which allowed him to reach for the telephone on the lamp table.

He ordered the continental breakfast: coffee, orange juice, fresh fruit and an assortment of toast and muffins.

When the line disconnected, he said, "Why don't you take the first shower. It might make you feel better."

"Actually, *you* made me feel better." She tossed him a smile that didn't quite light her eyes. "But I think I'll take you up on that."

Then she stood and walked to the bathroom.

He had a feeling that the nightmare was still eating at her, but he wasn't sure what else to do about it—other than suggest that they face the day head-on. So, while she was in the shower, he opened the blinds and took the time to watch dawn stretch over San Antonio.

A few minutes later, a knock sounded at the door. After slipping on the remaining robe, Jeremy answered.

"Where should I put this?" the bellman asked.

Jeremy nodded toward the coffee table in the living area. "Right over there."

While their meal was set up, Jeremy reached into his wallet and pulled out a couple bills to give the man, even though the gratuity had already been added into the tab.

"Can I get you anything else?" the man asked.

"No, thank you. This will be fine." After Jeremy signed the slip, the man left.

Rather than wait for Kirsten to come out of the shower, he poured a cup of coffee for himself.

Moments later, the bathroom door opened and she stepped out. Even with her wet hair wrapped in a towel turban, she looked like a million bucks.

His million bucks. He had a feeling he'd really struck pay dirt when he met her.

"Coffee?" he asked, as she joined him.

"Please." Kirsten took the cup Jeremy offered her, then added a splash of cream and sweetener before sitting next to him on the sofa.

The shower had done wonders.

And so had Jeremy.

Would another lover have been so thoughtful, so caring? So sweet?

She doubted it. So why was she apprehensive about sharing the uglier shades of her life with him?

There was no reason to feel that way. So she leveled with him and told him some of what Max had been going through with Courtney.

Jeremy didn't say anything right away. Finally, he set his cup on the table. "I find the whole story a little weird. Don't you?"

Weird?

Another sense of uneasiness washed over her, as she regretted airing her dirty laundry.

"What do you mean?" she asked.

"Your brother hadn't seen the woman in seven months, and she shows up at his door with a baby he didn't know he had. And according to you, he even questions whether he's the father."

Her tummy knotted. "I know he should have a

paternity test to answer that question, but I think it was admirable of him to take the baby."

"Yes, I can see why you might. But it's not clear if he has legal custody. What if there's a medical emergency?"

She supposed it was only natural that a physician would consider that. "I'm not sure what we'd do. I haven't thought that far yet. But little Anthony is a lot better off with Max than he is with Courtney."

"But he might not be Max's child."

She realized that. However, a parent didn't have to be related to a child by blood to offer it love and a happy home. "Maybe Max can become a foster parent or something." Anything that would allow him to keep the baby and not give him up to Courtney.

What kind of mother dropped off her child and never looked back?

"If Max is going to be working at the ranch during the day and going to school at nights, he's going to be hard-pressed to convince social services workers that he'd make a good foster parent."

The truth of Jeremy's statement stung. She wanted to tell him that she'd offer to be the foster parent, then. That she'd take the baby. But she bit back a response.

"And on top of that," Jeremy added, "she claimed that she doesn't have a birth certificate. Why is that?"

Kirsten didn't know why. Maybe she lost it. Or she moved before one could be mailed to her. Courtney had always been impulsive.

"It's anyone's guess," she said, although she couldn't

shake the feeling that her relationship with Jeremy had just turned south—or that it could easily go in that direction.

I find that a little weird, he'd said. *Don't you?*

Whose story was weird?

Courtney's? Or Kirsten's?

She reached for a muffin and carefully peeled back the paper, focusing on what was going into her mouth and not what was going on inside her heart.

In spite of what she'd thought, Jeremy wasn't a hundred percent supportive, when she'd really wanted him to be. When she'd really needed him to be.

And that put a damper on both the relationship and on the future.

Maybe she'd been wrong to think that she and Jeremy were having more than a brief affair. Instead he might only be looking for something temporary to fill his days before he headed back to California.

Besides, long-distance relationships didn't work very well, even if he was open to one. And if he asked her to relocate, she couldn't leave Anthony.

Not when she was the only one really looking out for him.

Jeremy spent the next night back at the Double Crown Ranch. His biggest reason for doing so was because he hated to leave Lily alone for a second day in a row. But he was also trying to decide how deep he wanted things to go with Kirsten, and he hoped that some time away from her might help him think.

So that was just what he'd done. But hell, she'd been on his mind constantly, and he was beginning to think that he was falling in love with her.

What else could it be?

As much as he'd told himself that he didn't believe in love at first sight, he would have to reconsider that belief because it sure seemed as if he'd started falling the moment he'd spotted her outside the clinic.

And after what they'd shared last night...

He ought to be concerned about the fact that she might have gotten pregnant, but for the life of him, it didn't seem like that big of a deal. Not if she wasn't worried about it.

They'd work through it, he supposed.

He had no idea what the future would bring. He was going to stay in Red Rock until he got word from—or *about*—his dad.

For the time being, he was settling in at the clinic and enjoying it a lot more than he thought he would. He'd even considered getting hospital privileges at the various medical centers in the area, although he hadn't done anything about it yet.

So much still hinged on his dad.

And on Kirsten, too—now that they'd struck up a relationship.

Ever since he'd checked them out of the hotel, he'd found himself wanting to be with her on a daily basis. And the drive back and forth from the Double Crown was a bit tiring.

Maybe he ought to get a place in town, just to be closer to her. But if he did, what about Lily?

Would she be okay without him to keep her company at night?

Dilemmas, he thought.

He glanced out the kitchen window, saw the morning sun peering over the eastern horizon. He was ready for a shot of caffeine to help him face the day, so he poured himself a cup of coffee.

While he pondered the situation with Kirsten and tried to connect all the dots, the housekeeper entered the kitchen.

"Excuse me, Dr. Fortune. But one of the ranch hands is at the front door. He'd like to talk to you."

"He wants to talk to *me?*" Had someone been injured? Jeremy tossed out the coffee in the sink. "Did he say what he wanted to see me about?"

"No, he didn't. But he did say that his name is Max. And that he's a friend of yours."

Uh-oh. What was wrong? Was the baby sick? Was something up with Kirsten?

Jeremy left his mug on the counter and headed for the back door, where he found Max waiting at the steps, holding his weathered hat in his hands.

His expression spelled trouble. "I'm sorry to bother you, but do you have a minute? I got here early, hoping I could talk to you before I have to check in with Ruben."

"Sure, I've got time to talk. Is something wrong?"

"Yeah. No." He lifted his battered Stetson, raked his

hair with his fingers, then returned the hat to his head. "Heck, I'm not sure. I've got a problem, and I didn't want to share it with Kirsten. We've been getting along a lot better lately, and I don't want her to get all weird on me."

"So you came to see me?"

"Yeah. I hope you don't mind."

"No problem." Actually, Jeremy thought it was a good sign that Max was seeking wise counsel—assuming that was what he'd come for.

"That's good, because I really need a man's perspective on this. Kirsten gets way too emotionally involved in this kind of stuff."

"Women tend to be that way," Jeremy said. "But I think it might make for a good balance."

"Maybe."

"Want to take a walk?"

Max nodded. "Yeah, that might help."

Jeremy closed the door, then followed Max down the steps and out into the yard.

"You know," Max said, "if my old man was still around, I'd talk to him. But he bailed out on me a long time ago."

"I'm glad you came to me, then. Sometimes it helps to talk it out."

Max didn't speak right away, but Jeremy kept quiet, biding his time until Max was ready to open up.

Finally, he said, "I'm not sure how much you know about all of this, but my old girlfriend Courtney showed up at the house, telling me that Anthony was mine."

"Kirsten mentioned it."

"She wanted me to take care of him because she couldn't."

"Does she want him back?" Jeremy asked.

"No, that's not the problem."

Jeremy wanted to press for more details, but continued to hold back, waiting for Max to explain in his own time.

"Even when Courtney brought Anthony to me," he finally said, "I had my doubts about whether I was his father or not. But how could I tell her I wouldn't take the poor little guy? I mean, he's just a baby. And I knew he'd be better off with me and Kirsten."

Jeremy assumed he was right about that.

"Courtney and I had a thing going for a while, but we split up for a good reason. She's a real flake."

Jeremy wasn't about to comment on that. Especially when he had no reason to doubt Max.

"I talked to her last night, after Kirsten went to bed. And it seems that I was right. I'm not Anthony's father."

So she was messing around on Max? And then she had the gall to dump her kid on him?

Flakey didn't seem to describe her as well as a few other choice adjectives might. But Jeremy kept that to himself as well, choosing to let Max continue.

"It seems that his father is some guy named Charlie," Max said. "And apparently, he's bad news. Somehow, he found out that Anthony is with me, although he has no idea where to find me."

Maybe not yet. But if he ever did locate Max, Kirsten would be in danger, which sent every one of Jeremy's instincts on high alert.

An almost overwhelming urge to drive into Red Rock and protect her slammed into him.

"What kind of 'bad news' is this guy?" Jeremy asked.

"She wouldn't tell me. She just begged me to keep Anthony safe. And she seemed to think that he would be, as long as we had him."

"We," of course, meant Kirsten and Max.

"Did you tell your sister any of this?"

"Not yet. I thought it would be best if I talked to you about it first. All I need is for Kirsten to come unglued. And she would. She's a real mother hen. And she's gotten pretty attached to Anthony."

Jeremy had noticed that, too. But he didn't want to see Kirsten in any trouble—or in danger—if that Charlie guy came looking for his son.

"So what should I do?" Max asked.

"I think it's time for you to go to the police. Now that you know you're not his father, you have no legal right to keep him. And you could actually end up in trouble for harboring a child who isn't yours."

"Dang." Max bit his lip. "I don't want any problems like that."

Jeremy glanced at his wristwatch. "What time do you need to start work?"

"I can't stick around here. I've got to tell Kirsten what's going on. And then I need to talk to the police."

Ruben would probably understand, but Jeremy thought it would be best if Max stayed on the job and put in an honest day's work, especially since Jeremy could handle the rest.

He could also make sure that Kirsten was safe.

"You stay here. I'll give Kirsten the news and let her know what you've decided."

"You don't mind?"

"Not a bit. Thanks for trusting me."

"How could I not do that? You've always been straight with me. And you've been looking out for my best interests, even though you don't know me all that well."

No, but Jeremy knew his sister. And that had been good enough for him.

He just hoped that Courtney hadn't involved Max and Kirsten in a dangerous situation.

Chapter Eleven

Making love with Jeremy the night before last had been both unimaginable and spellbinding.

Yet Kirsten couldn't help thinking that he was pulling away from her. After all, he'd taken her home after they'd stayed in San Antonio, then had gone to the clinic to work. But instead of stopping by her house when he was done, he'd gone to the ranch.

He'd said that he needed to check on Lily, and that was probably true—and admirable, of course. Still, Kirsten couldn't help thinking that he might be having second thoughts.

So last night, when she'd pulled back the covers and slid into her bed alone, she'd closed her eyes and tried to imagine his smiling face, the way the sun picked up strands of gold in his hair.

The image she liked most, though, was the one of him stretched out on the bed beside her, his hand resting on her hip, his mouth trailing down her neck and pausing to kiss her breasts.

She'd wanted to sleep the night away just so she could remain in a dream world.

The phone rang at eight the next morning, finally jarring her back to reality.

She squinted as she reached for the receiver on the nightstand, then cleared her throat before answering. "Hello?"

"Kirsten Allen?" an unfamiliar voice asked.

"Yes."

"This is Stacy Grabowski, with the Fortune Foundation. We're looking for an accountant, and I was wondering if you'd like to come in for a job interview."

She'd never applied there, although she wouldn't mind working for the organization. Her first thought was that Jeremy must have had something to do with it. Yet instead of shooting a pleasant thrill through her, the idea left her uneasy.

Did that mean taking her to California was out of the question?

Sadly, it seemed to be the only logical explanation, yet she still felt compelled to ask. "How did you get my name?"

"Fred Nettles, who works in human resources for Alliance Plumbing, is one of our board members. He received the job application and résumé you sent to his company a few weeks back. They were in the process of hiring someone else, but he knew we were looking for someone, too. Since he was impressed with your qualifications, he suggested we interview you."

So her name coming up for that particular position had been a coincidence? Something that came about without Jeremy's recommendation?

Stacy went on to give Kirsten more details and provide a job description, all of which would utilize the skills she'd acquired. In fact, it was right up her alley.

To top it off, the benefits were in line with what she'd been hoping to get, and the starting salary was better yet. So it sounded as though the position would be perfect for her.

She wasn't sure how she'd juggle things, though. Max was going to need a lot of help with Anthony. But if they both had jobs, day care would be affordable.

Part of her insisted that she stay home with the baby until he was older, but how could she tell the Fortune Foundation no? She might never get another chance to work for them again.

There was, of course, the hope that her relationship with Jeremy would work out and become much more involved. But there were no guarantees there, either.

So why put her job search on hold indefinitely?

Besides, she might not even land the position.

And to make matters worse, she had to admit that some of the things Jeremy had said while they'd been at the hotel had been true. If Max wasn't Anthony's legal guardian, Courtney could show up at anytime, wanting him back. And unless Kirsten was prepared for a big legal battle, she'd have to give him up.

Again, she worried about letting him go, but even *that* was still up in the air. So she told Stacy, "Sure, I'd like to come in for an interview."

They'd no more than agreed to a date and a time when Anthony woke up—cranky and hungry, no doubt. So she hung up the phone and went to get the baby out of his Portacrib.

"I'm here, honey. Let me get your bottle." With Anthony resting in the crook of her arms, she padded into the kitchen to mix his powdered formula with water. Then she carried him into the living room, where she sat in the recliner and placed the nipple in his mouth.

As he ate, she watched him gulp and swallow. Every once in a while, he'd look at her, release his hold on the nipple and grin, which sent a dribble of milk down his chin. It was so sweet. And it let her know that he recognized her, that they were connected in some special way.

In just over a week, she'd really grown attached to the little guy. She'd love to keep him, to adopt him, to become a mother to him legally. Yet she also knew that she might have to give him up. But as long as she handed him over to parents who were kind and loving, she'd be okay with that.

She just couldn't stand the idea of letting Courtney take him back.

Kirstin had made a promise to herself—and to

the baby. She would do whatever she could to protect Anthony.

No matter what.

Thanks to another long-distance consultation with a colleague in his Sacramento medical group that tied him up for an hour, Jeremy wasn't able to get to Kirsten's house until just after eight. As concerned as he was for her safety, Max had convinced him that it wouldn't be easy for Charlie to find Anthony in Red Rock.

So he parked at the curb, then rang the bell.

When the door swung open, Kirsten was wearing a pale blue bathrobe and holding Anthony in her arms.

"I'm sorry to stop by so early," he said, "but I wanted to talk to you."

"I was just going to make some coffee," she said, stepping aside to let him into her cozy living room. "Can I get you a cup?"

"No, thanks. As much as I'd like to, I can't stay long. I need to get to the clinic, but I have to talk to you about something important."

She looked a little pale, a little uneasy. "What is it?"

"Max talked to me this morning."

Her brow furrowed. "He called *you?* Whatever for?"

"He didn't call. He showed up early at the ranch and asked for my advice about a problem he has."

"Is he feeling okay?" she asked.

He supposed it was only natural that she'd think his

reason to talk to a doctor would be a medical issue. "No, he isn't sick."

"Then what did he want to talk to you about?"

"About the latest call he got from Courtney." Jeremy filled her in on the details, adding, "According to her, she lied about Max being Anthony's father. Instead, it's a guy named Charlie."

"I don't understand," Kirsten said. "Why would she lie about that? And who is Charlie? Was she seeing him before she and my brother broke up?"

"I'm not sure. But from what Courtney told your brother, Charlie isn't a nice guy."

"Oh, God." Kirsten drew the baby closer to her chest, then slowly dropped into an overstuffed chair. "Are you sure about that?"

"No, that's just it. Courtney's stories aren't consistent. And she's repeatedly lied. So Max can't tell what's true and what's fabricated."

Kirsten looked down at the baby she held, the child who was totally dependent on her. It didn't take a mind reader to know what she was thinking. She was worried about little Anthony, and she had good reason to be. His mother was unstable, and his father was of questionable character.

As far as Jeremy was concerned, there was only one thing to do. They had to contact the police.

"According to Courtney," Jeremy added, "Charlie knows the baby is with Max. So it's just a matter of time before he finds him and Anthony."

And before he found Kirsten, too. Jeremy's chest

tightened at the thought that she might be in the thick of it all.

What if Charlie proved to be unpredictable? Courtney certainly was.

Kirsten furrowed her brow, apparently trying to sort through the news she'd been given, then looked up. "Maybe Max should stay out on the ranch for a while. Is that possible?"

"If Charlie comes around, he won't be looking for your brother. He'll be looking for his son."

"Then I'll keep Anthony under the radar," she said. "And if Charlie doesn't know to look for him here…"

"Be reasonable, Kirsten. If Charlie comes looking for Max and the baby here, you might not be safe." And for that reason, Jeremy had packed his clothes with the intention of staying with her until things could be sorted out, although he'd left them in the car.

"Then maybe I ought to leave for a while."

"And go where?" he said.

"I don't know. A hotel. Someplace."

Jeremy blew out a sigh. Why couldn't she wrap her mind around the situation?

"You *can't* keep Anthony," he explained. "He's not your baby, and you don't have any legal claim to him."

Her eyes flashed, challenging him. "I don't care about that. I won't give him up to someone who won't take care of him, someone who can't give him the love that he deserves."

"You might not have a choice," Jeremy countered. "Besides, you may not want to believe this, but there are a lot of kids in this world who aren't loved and taken care of. I see them all the time at the clinic with sad eyes, broken arms, bruises—"

"Stop! I'm aware of that. It sickens me to think about kids being neglected and abused. And you're right. I can't save them from the brutal reality they live with day to day. But I *can* protect Anthony. And I will. I'm not going to let anything happen to him. If that means hiding out with him and not telling anyone I've got him, then that's fine."

"You're being foolish, Kirsten. And you're also risking your own safety, not to mention the baby's."

"Not if no one knows where to find him."

"Oh, for Pete's sake. Courtney knows exactly where he is. And she can't be trusted."

The truth of Jeremy's statement slammed into Kirsten, backing her into a corner, it seemed. But what else could she do?

Her heart sank, but not just out of fear for herself. "If Charlie proves to be dangerous, and if you think that I'm not safe, then how can I let Anthony go with him?"

"You're right. That's why we need to go to the police and let them deal with it."

Kirsten cuddled the baby closer yet, unwilling to let law enforcement step in. Weren't they bound by law to hand Anthony over to his biological parents?

"What do you think your brother will have to say about this?" Jeremy asked.

"It really doesn't matter, does it? If Max isn't Anthony's father, then he can just stay out of it."

"But Max is already involved."

"How do you figure?"

"Come on. Open your eyes, Kirsten. Look beyond the child in your arms and face the larger picture. Max doesn't know any of the details surrounding that baby. What if Charlie *isn't* 'bad news'? What if, for some reason, he was granted legal custody, and Courtney took him away? After all, if she's as unstable as she seems to be, then who knows what's really going on?"

He was right, Kirsten realized. But she couldn't shake the feeling that Anthony wasn't safe unless he was with her. "I appreciate your concern, but I can't call the police. Not yet."

Jeremy chuffed, then muttered, "What a convoluted mess. I can't believe I'm even involved in this."

Kirsten had always been afraid that Jeremy would bail out if Max's drama ever got to be too much for him, so his comment crushed her. But how could she turn her back on the baby now?

Silence stretched between them. And as the minutes ticked by, she threw out the only argument she had left. "Apparently, you don't know what it means to love someone, Jeremy. To be committed to them."

His eye twitched, and his mouth tensed. She'd clearly angered him, and while she hated to think that her love for Anthony had driven them apart, she couldn't help it. He was a helpless little baby, for goodness' sake.

"You're wrong," Jeremy finally said. "I *do* know what

it means to love someone, to want them to be safe and happy. And it frustrates the hell out of me to see her refuse to see reason and to dig in her heels about the simplest thing."

Was he talking about his feelings for *her?*

She thought he might be, but she wasn't sure.

Taking a gamble, she said, "I love you, Jeremy. But you can't ask me to choose between my family and you."

He threw up his hands, clearly frustrated with her, with the situation, with the stalemate they'd reached.

"Maybe you'd better go," she said, wishing he'd have a change of heart, that he would soften with time. That he would be as supportive of her as he was when he found her awake and stewing over the nightmare she'd had—the nightmare about Anthony being in danger.

"Maybe I should." He turned and let himself out of the house.

She wanted to stop him, to try to explain. But what more was there to say?

As she stood at the living-room window and watched him climb into his car, she prayed that he was the one who would see reason. That he'd come back to her.

And that he wouldn't go to the authorities himself.

Apparently, you don't know what it means to love someone.

When Jeremy left Kirsten's house, the words she'd thrown at him stung something fierce.

The hell he didn't know what it meant to love someone.

He loved *her*. And the thought of something happening to *her* was making him crazy.

In fact, he was fit to be tied. How could she be so irrational about all of this?

If he had any sense at all, he'd go to the clinic to work, then head back to the Double Crown and call it a day, but he couldn't do that. He was too caught up in the situation.

But he wasn't too caught up to realize that there might be legal ramifications for what Kirsten planned to do. And he couldn't let her make a mistake like that.

So after calling the clinic and letting them know he would be coming in late, he drove to San Antonio, where Rafe Mendoza had opened his new law office.

Rafe wasn't just a friend. He was also family, related to Jeremy by marriage—his half-sister, Isabella, had married Jeremy's brother J.R. And if there was anyone Jeremy could trust to provide sound legal counsel, it was the attorney in San Antonio's newest law firm.

Hopefully, Rafe wouldn't be too busy to see him.

After leaving his car in the underground parking structure, Jeremy took the elevator to the lobby, where he talked to the security personnel, identified himself, then waited for permission to proceed to the elevator.

Rafe's office was located on the fifth floor and overlooked the River Walk. In fact, it wasn't too far from the hotel in which Jeremy and Kirsten had spent the night.

Just being in the area was a nice reminder of what they'd shared together, of what the future might hold if things worked out. And that was why it was important for him to make sure that Kirsten didn't get into any trouble.

When Jeremy finally entered the reception area of Rafe's office, he strode to the legal assistant's desk. "Hello, Vonda. Is Rafe available?"

"I believe so. Let me tell him you're here."

While she paged her boss, Jeremy shoved his hands in his pockets and scanned the spacious office, noting the expensive dark wood and the leather furnishings, as well as an expanse of windows that provided a nice view of the river.

At only twenty-nine years of age, Rafe was doing pretty well for himself these days. He already had a successful law practice in Ann Arbor. And he'd just recently returned to Texas to open a second office.

One of the many things Jeremy appreciated about Rafe was his air of confidence, which made him a good attorney.

Moments later, the handsome, dark-haired man entered the waiting area and reached out his hand to greet Jeremy. "It's good to see you. Did you come by to welcome me back to Texas?"

"Actually, I wanted to discuss a legal issue with you."

Rafe's mood grew serious. "Sure, come with me. Let's talk about it in private."

Once they'd each taken a seat, Jeremy couldn't help noting the glass case that held a variety of trophies and team photos from Rafe's years of playing baseball through high school and college.

"You've got a nice office," he told the well-built athlete who dressed in power suits these days.

"Thanks."

Minutes later, Jeremy had told Rafe about Kirsten, Max and Anthony.

"I'd like to help," Rafe said, "but I'm a corporate attorney and this really isn't my field. I can refer you to a specialist, though."

"I'm not ready to discuss this with anyone else. So even though you're not all that up on family law, you should have an opinion that would be helpful."

"I can do that," Rafe said. "But it seems to me that the first thing to do is to request the birth certificate."

"That's the problem. Courtney, the baby's mother, doesn't seem to have it. Or, if she does, she's not making it readily available. And God only knows who fathered Anthony. She first told Max that the baby was his. Now she's saying the father is someone named Charlie."

"It sounds like a real mess."

Jeremy nodded. "You've got that right. In Kirsten's defense, she only has the baby's best interests at heart. But I'm afraid she's setting herself up for trouble if she doesn't call the police and report the situation."

"I agree," Rafe said. "Who knows what the actual details are? It could even be a noncustodial kidnapping. Maybe Courtney considers Charlie 'bad news' because he's furious at her for leaving and wants his son back."

"That thought crossed my mind, too." And if that was the case, Charlie wouldn't pose a threat to anyone other than Courtney. Hoping for the best, yet not convinced,

Jeremy blew out a sigh. "So you would advise her to report it."

"Well, that's the correct legal move," Rafe said. "But you should probably keep in mind that Kirsten's emotions are involved. And under the circumstance, doing the 'right' thing could prove costly to *you*."

Jeremy suspected that Rafe meant he could win the battle and lose the girl, which would hurt. But he couldn't stand by and watch Kirsten make a mistake that would cost them both a whole lot more.

Rafe added, "It sounds to me as though Kirsten is the type who would sacrifice her own comfort—maybe even her freedom—to keep her family safe."

For a moment, Jeremy wondered if Rafe was speaking from experience, although he was probably reading too much into his tone, into his words. Either way, he didn't question him.

"I guess I'll have to really give it some thought," he said instead.

"I would." Rafe sat back in the desk chair. "Just how important is this woman to you?"

Jeremy hated to admit it, but he leveled with his friend. "Kirsten's come to mean a great deal to me."

In fact, Kirsten was proving to be a real mama bear when she thought one of her cubs was in danger—just like Molly Fortune had been. And he had to give her credit for that.

It was, he supposed, the result of thinking with her heart instead of her head. And it reminded him of the words he'd had with Max just a few hours earlier.

When Max complained that Kirsten got way too emotionally involved in things, Jeremy had said getting emotionally involved was a trait many women had. And that it made for a "good balance" in a relationship.

He probably ought to keep that in mind.

After thanking Rafe for his time, he stood to leave. "Have Vonda send me a bill. I'm staying at the Double Crown."

"No," Rafe said. "I won't be charging you anything. This one's on me. Besides, this really isn't my specialty."

"I needed some sound advice, and you gave it to me. So thanks again. I owe you one."

As Jeremy headed for his car, he realized he would have to go along with Kirsten's wishes for now. But that didn't mean he wasn't worried.

Instead of heading to the clinic, he drove back to Kirsten's house, hoping to set things to rights.

But when he arrived, his heart dropped to the ground when he knocked and rang the bell, only to find her gone.

Chapter Twelve

Jeremy tried to tell himself that Kirsten was probably at the grocery store or running errands, but that didn't quell his worry.

After ringing the bell and knocking on the front door numerous times, he peered through the small window into the garage, only to see that her car was gone. At least, she wasn't sitting inside, refusing to see him.

So now what?

He'd be damned if he'd just head to the clinic, go to work and pretend as if nothing was wrong. Maybe he ought to hang out here for a while and wait to see if she came home.

Or better yet, he should try her on her cell. But before he could dial out, a call came in.

He answered without checking the display. "Hello?"

"Jeremy? It's Ruben. Your buddy Max didn't show up this morning. Do you have any idea why?"

He didn't show up? "What do you mean? He was at the ranch early this morning. I talked to him."

"Then he must have left before I started lining up the hands for the day."

Damn. This whole thing was blowing up in Jeremy's face.

"Listen, Ruben. I don't know what's going on, but I'll get to the bottom of it. And as soon as I do, I'll give you a call."

When the line disconnected, Jeremy swore under his breath. Then he dialed Kirsten's number. He let out another curse when he reached her voice mail, but went ahead and left a message, asking her to call as soon as she got it.

But where the hell was she? And why did Max take off this morning after Jeremy told him to go to work?

He glanced at his wristwatch. It was Anthony's nap time. So why wasn't Kirsten home? And why wasn't she picking up the damn phone?

His first thought was to do what he'd wanted to do originally, and that was to call the police. But out of respect and courtesy to Kirsten, he held back—at least momentarily. However, if she was in trouble, if Charlie had come around, if…

Jeremy raked his hand through his hair, then tried her number again. Finally, when he was about to disconnect, she picked up, her voice distraught.

"Jeremy?" she asked.

"Yes, it's me. Where are you?"

"I'm driving around town, looking for Max. He came home right after you left my house. He told me that he didn't have to work today after all. So I asked him to watch Anthony while I ran to the market. He agreed, but when I got back, he and the baby were gone. He also took the diaper bag, the supply of bottles and formula and the Portacrib. I have no idea where he went or what he plans to do."

"Have you called him?"

"Several times, but his phone must be shut off. Either that or the battery is dead. I'm really getting worried."

"Where are you now?" Jeremy asked.

"I'm sitting in my car. I pulled over by that new burger place when you called."

"Then come home. I'll be waiting for you. And we'll figure this out together."

Ten minutes later, Kirsten arrived at the house. Her eyes were red-rimmed, her cheeks tearstained.

"You were right all along," she said. "We should have gone to the police. But oh, no, I wouldn't listen. And now Max and the baby are gone."

"Did he say anything to you earlier about where he might go and why? Maybe he was afraid that Charlie found out where you lived. Maybe he's trying to protect you and the baby."

"Oh, my God. Do you think that's what happened?"

"I have no idea. Right now, I'm just grabbing at straws. But it doesn't matter. We'll find them, honey. I promise we will. And we don't have to alert the authorities unless you want to."

Kirsten looked at him, confusion etched across her face. "I don't understand. You were gung ho to call them earlier. Why the change of heart?"

He slipped his arms around her. "I haven't changed my mind. I still think we would be better off going the legal route. But I love you enough to trust that you'll do the right thing when you're ready."

"You *love* me?" She seemed awed, touched. Surprised.

"Yes, I do." He kissed her, his lips lingering over hers for the longest time, his heart fully engaged.

Just as they drew apart, Kirsten's cell phone rang.

"It could be Max," she said, flipping open the lid. "I need to take it."

"Kirsten?" Max said.

When Kirsten heard her brother's voice over the line, her breath caught.

"Where are you?" she asked. "And where is the baby?"

"Anthony's with me. And we're both safe."

Relief flooded through her. "Tell me where you are. If you don't want to come home, at least let me keep the baby for you."

"Can I talk to Jeremy first?"

Before answering her question? Before telling her where he was? She wanted to throttle him, but she handed over the cell to Jeremy anyway.

She supposed she ought to be glad that Max respected the man enough to go to him for sage advice, something that had been sorely lacking in his life since their father left. So she swallowed back her hurt feelings and homed in on the one side of the conversation she could hear.

"What's going on?" Jeremy asked, listening intently. Then he said, "You've got to be kidding me."

What? Kirsten wanted to ask, moving closer, hoping to catch a word or a phrase of whatever explanation Max was giving him.

"You're going to have to stop calling her a flake," Jeremy said. "That doesn't even begin to describe her or her character."

The conversation continued, but Jeremy only uttered a grunt now and then. And by the time he ended the call, Kirsten was beside herself.

"What's that crazy woman done now?" she asked.

"You aren't going to believe this. She just told Max that she's not the baby's mother."

Kirsten was stunned. "Then who's his mom?" she asked. "And where did Courtney get him?"

"She insists that she didn't kidnap him. And she still claims that Charlie is the father, that he left him with her."

Kirsten's head was spinning, and her heart was breaking. That precious little child didn't deserve any of this. God only knew who his real parents were.

"Where are Max and Anthony now?" she finally asked.

"Max is taking the baby to the police department. He said the baby was entrusted to him, and that it's his responsibility to do the right thing."

"What does that mean?"

"He's decided to take the advice I gave him earlier and is going to report this to the police."

"Then we need to meet him there." For a moment, Kirsten feared that Jeremy would remind her that he had to go to the clinic this morning, that he was too busy to get involved, especially in this kind of mess.

But he did just as she'd hoped he would. He slipped an arm around her shoulders and said, "Yes, we do. Get Anthony's car seat, and we'll put it in my vehicle. When I told you we were in this together, I meant it."

Kirsten didn't think she could love the man any more than she did right now.

Ten minutes later, Jeremy drove Kirsten and Max to the police precinct.

"What if they take him away from us?" she asked. "I hate the idea of Anthony going with strangers."

It was better than having the mysterious Charlie find him, Jeremy thought. Besides, Anthony was young enough that he'd probably be okay with anyone who kept him warm and fed, anyone who was loving and kind. But he didn't share that thought with Kirsten.

As far as she was concerned, no one could take care of Anthony as well as she could. And Jeremy had to agree with that.

"Don't worry. I'll do whatever it takes to convince the authorities to let us keep him until things get sorted out."

"Us?" she asked, her eyes hopeful and bright.

"Yes, *us.* We're in this together, honey. And I plan to call in some favors. The Fortunes and the Mendozas are highly thought of in these parts. So I don't think you have anything to worry about."

At least, not yet.

Once at police headquarters, Max told the officer in charge why they were there. Then they were taken to a small conference room, where Max reported all that he knew about Charlie and Courtney.

The officer in charge leaned back in his chair. "We'll place the baby in protective custody while we track down the parents."

"We'd like to keep him with us," Jeremy said. "We've got a bedroom for him. And we've been taking care of him for weeks."

"I don't mind placing the child with family," the officer said, "but under the circumstances…"

"I'm a physician," Jeremy said, giving Max a look and a silent message to encourage him to follow his lead. "And this is my fiancée and her brother."

Kirsten didn't say a word, although she tensed a bit at his response. So he took her hand in his and gave it a warm, trust-me-honey squeeze.

"The baby will be much better off with us," he added. "We've also got a list of references, beginning with J. R. Fortune and Jose Mendoza. You won't be sorry."

Jeremy watched as Max began to nod in agreement and as a grin spread over his face. It was clear that he understood what Jeremy was trying to make happen.

Getting the authorities to award temporary custody to Max might have been a stretch, but a solid and dependable couple stood a lot better chance.

The officer thought about it a moment, then said, "I'll have to run it by a judge so that we can get a temporary custody order. Hold on while I see if I can find one who's nearby and available."

When the man stepped out of the room, Max said, "Anthony needs a diaper change. And there's one of those family restrooms just down the hall. I'll be right back."

When they were alone, Kirsten nudged Jeremy's arm. "Your *fiancée?*"

"I thought it might help sway the judge to grant you custody."

Kirsten's brow furrowed, and her expression grew serious. "You're probably right, but I…"

He wasn't sure what was bothering her, the fact that he'd stretched the truth about an engagement, he supposed. But this wasn't a discussion he wanted to have at the courthouse. "We can talk more about it later."

She nodded, yet her apprehension remained.

Twenty minutes later, it was official. Kirsten Allen and Dr. Jeremy Fortune had temporary legal custody of Baby Anthony Doe.

With everything in order, they headed for the car to make the short drive back to Kirsten's house.

"Thanks so much for all you've done for me and my

sister," Max said. "This situation has been pretty tough on us, but having you in our corner sure helped."

"I'm glad everything worked out."

"I'd better give Ruben a call," Max added. "I need to apologize for taking off like I did, but when Courtney said she was leaving the area and that she wanted to meet with me before she went, I didn't know what else to do."

"Hopefully Ruben will cut you some slack," Jeremy said. "But next time something like that happens, you're going to have to level with him—or with whoever your supervisor happens to be. You can't just walk off a job site without an explanation."

"I'll remember that."

"So where did Courtney go?" Kirsten asked.

"She wouldn't tell me. But she did give me this." Max reached into his pocket, pulled out a small gold medallion and dropped it in his sister's hand.

"What is it?" Kirsten asked, as she studied the golden coin in her palm.

"Courtney said that Anthony was wearing it when Charlie gave him to her."

Jeremy studied the medallion. "It doesn't look all that expensive. But maybe it holds a clue as to who he is and where he belongs."

He sure hoped so. They could all stand a few answers right now.

* * *

Meanwhile, miles away in a small Texas town, a teenager hanging out at a bus stop spotted an old homeless guy wandering the streets. At least, he looked homeless. He also appeared to be disoriented, maybe strung out on something.

When he approached the bench, where the kid sat, he furrowed his silver brow—confused, it seemed.

He had to be in his late sixties or early seventies. Heck, maybe even older.

As he scanned the immediate area, the bench, the grass, the sidewalk—even the sky—it was pretty obvious that he didn't have any idea where he was.

"You okay?" the kid asked him.

"I'm not sure."

"What's your name?" the boy asked.

Confusion washed over his bearded face. "I...I don't know."

The teen wondered if he ought to report the old guy, although he seemed harmless. Just a little messed up, which was really sad for a guy his age. He ought to be sitting in a rocking chair on a porch somewhere, not wandering around and scrounging for a meal.

Feeling especially sympathetic, the kid reached into his pocket and retrieved a granola bar he'd grabbed from the kitchen pantry on his way out of the house today. "You want this?"

The old guy took it, rolled it over. Then he looked up and smiled wistfully. "Thanks."

"You're welcome."

The kid didn't smell stale booze or smoke on him, but who knew for sure. So he asked, "You a wino? Or maybe a druggie?"

The man slowly shook his head. "No, but to tell you the truth, I feel kind of hungover. Maybe I was at a frat party."

At *his* age? And in *his* condition? No way.

The guy was clearly whacked-out. Maybe he was one of those Alzheimer's patients who wandered away from the nursing home every now and then.

"How old are you?" the kid asked.

"Twenty-five," he said. "Or maybe twenty-six. I forget."

Oh, yeah? Then he must have forgotten about fifty whole years of his life.

"Why don't you sit down on that bench," the kid said. "I'll see if I can get you some aspirin or something for your hangover. Or better yet, I'll call someone to come get you and take you to a clinic."

"No," the old man said. "I'll be fine. It's just that I have something to do. Something very important."

"What's that?" the kid asked.

"I... I'm not sure."

The kid looked up and down the street. Where were the cops when you really needed one?

He was just about to call 911, when his cell phone chimed. His buddy D.J. was texting him, so he flipped to the screen to read the message.

A couple of their friends were going to a movie and D.J. asked if he wanted to join them.

He glanced at the old man. Why did he think it was his job to help? There were a lot of other people around—adults who were better able to deal with the poor guy's issues than he was. So he decided to take off and find his friends.

"You take care," he said. "Okay, dude?"

The old man looked up, just as confused as ever.

Back at the Double Crown Ranch, Lily put on a kettle of water to boil. Then she removed a china cup from the cupboard and took a box of chamomile tea from the pantry.

The phone rang, and she answered.

"Lily," Jeremy said. "If all goes according to plan, I'll be staying at Kirsten's tonight, so I won't be coming home. Are you going to be okay?"

"I'm fine," she said.

Jeremy had always been a sweet boy, and she knew that he'd been staying with her to keep her company until William returned. "Thanks for letting me know."

Silence stretched across the line until Jeremy said, "I worry about you when I'm not there. I have a feeling you're just waiting for the telephone to ring with news of my dad."

"The waiting isn't in vain."

Jeremy didn't respond right away. Then he asked, "Have you heard from the police lately? Have they uncovered anything else?"

Not anything of substance. "No, but I'm sure it's just a matter of time. We'll hear something soon."

As the kettle went off, she turned down the fire. "Why don't you bring Kirsten out here for dinner tomorrow night?"

"I'd like that, Lily."

"Good. Dinner will be ready at six, but you can come whenever you like."

"Thanks." He paused again, then added, "Are you sure you'll be okay without me home tonight?"

"Absolutely. I'm not alone." He probably thought that she meant her household staff and the ranch hands were nearby, but she couldn't help thinking that it was more than that.

"Take care," he said. "And sleep tight."

"I will. Kiss Kirsten and that baby for me. I'll see you tomorrow."

When the call ended, she filled her cup with hot water, then dropped a chamomile tea bag into it.

As she waited for it to steep, she sensed a presence—just like she had several times before.

She couldn't explain it—that warm, inner peace. The sense of calm, of love.

Nor could she shake the words that seemed to speak to her mind.

"Don't give up hope," they whispered. "He'll come home to you."

She nodded, as if she could somehow communicate right back.

I won't give up. I'll wait for him until the day I die.

* * *

When Jeremy had called Kirsten his fiancée at the courthouse, her heart had sung with hope.

But when she quizzed him about his comment, he'd said, "I thought it might help sway the judge to grant you custody."

At that point, her song had hit a flat note.

Not that she didn't appreciate what Jeremy had done to ensure that she would get custody of Anthony. But his lie had only opened a new can of worms, and she couldn't help worrying that there might be some legal ramifications if the court ever learned that they weren't really engaged.

He'd told her that he loved her, of course. But he'd never mentioned anything about a commitment.

"We can talk more about it later," he'd said.

But as luck would have it, Anthony had been fussy on the short ride back to her house, and Jeremy had been tightlipped.

Then he'd disappeared for a while, saying he was going to pick up groceries so he could fix dinner for her this evening.

Maybe they would finally have a chance to talk about the future while they ate. She sure hoped so. Not knowing what he was thinking or feeling made her more than a little uneasy.

And to top it off, Jeremy had gone into the kitchen more than an hour ago and had refused to let her in while he cooked.

"It's a surprise," he'd said, each time she'd knocked at the door.

She wasn't sure what he was making, but it certainly smelled delicious.

So, after bathing Anthony and putting on his onesie, Kirsten gave him a bottle and put him to bed. Then she waited on the sofa for Jeremy to announce that everything was ready.

Max, who'd taken a shower and splashed on a bit of his favorite aftershave, entered the living room, dressed to the hilt in a new pair of jeans and a plaid flannel shirt.

He'd been invited to Kelly's house again, which meant Jeremy and Kirsten would have a quiet night alone.

"Don't wait up for me," Max said. "And go ahead and lock the door whenever you decide to turn in. I have a key, but I have a feeling I'll be invited to stay over for breakfast, too."

He was grinning from ear to ear, and Kirsten couldn't help being happy for him.

"Drive carefully," she said.

"I always do."

After Max left, she reached for the novel she'd left on the lamp table and opened to the bookmarked page. But she didn't read more than a paragraph before Jeremy stepped through the doorway, his eyes lit up like a child's at Christmas.

"Dinner's ready," he said.

"Good." She returned the book to the table, then got to her feet.

"Before we eat," he said, "I have something I want to ask you."

"What's that?"

He crossed the room and took her by the hand. Then he dropped to one knee.

Her imagination, as well as her heart, began to race, but she feared that she might be jumping to the wrong conclusion.

"What are you doing?"

He reached into his pocket, pulled out a small, Tiffany-blue-colored box and popped open the lid, revealing the biggest, shiniest diamond she'd ever seen.

"Will you marry me, Kirsten?"

Her heart dropped to the pit of her stomach, then began to rumble back into her chest. She opened her mouth to speak, but the words wouldn't form.

"Is this for real?" she finally asked.

He cocked his head slightly to the side, and his smile faded. "What do you mean?"

"An engagement," she said. "Is it real? Or is it just a part of your plan to sway the judge?"

A grin tugged at his lips. "If you say no, then I'll claim it was only part of that particular plan. But the truth is, I love you, Kirsten. And I want to marry you—judge or no judge."

Tears welled in her eyes. She tried to blink them back, but wasn't having any luck. She knew she should respond to his proposal, but the emotion, the happiness, the dreams of a wonderful future all tumbled around in her throat.

"Aren't you going to say anything?" he asked.

"Yes!" she finally said through tears. "I'll marry you. And I'll follow you to California or Timbuktu. It doesn't matter to me, as long as we're together."

Then she pulled him to his feet, threw her arms around his neck and kissed him with all the love in her heart.

The future might be a little uncertain at the moment, Kirsten decided, but it had never looked brighter.

* * * * *

Don't miss Mendoza's Return,
the next book in
THE FORTUNES OF TEXAS:
LOST...AND FOUND.
Coming next month from
Silhouette Special Edition.

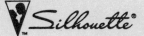
Silhouette®

COMING NEXT MONTH

Available February 22, 2011

SPECIAL EDITION

#2101 MARRIAGE, BRAVO STYLE!
Christine Rimmer
Bravo Family Ties

#2102 MENDOZA'S RETURN
Susan Crosby
The Fortunes of Texas: Lost...and Found

#2103 TAMING THE TEXAS PLAYBOY
Crystal Green
Billionaire Cowboys, Inc.

#2104 HIS TEXAS WILDFLOWER
Stella Bagwell
Men of the West

#2105 SOMETHING UNEXPECTED
Wendy Warren
Home Sweet Honeyford

#2106 THE MILLIONAIRE'S WISH
Abigail Strom

SSECNM0211

REQUEST YOUR FREE BOOKS!

2 FREE NOVELS PLUS 2 FREE GIFTS!

SPECIAL EDITION
Life, Love and Family!

YES! Please send me 2 FREE Silhouette Special Edition® novels and my 2 FREE gifts (gifts are worth about $10). After receiving them, if I don't wish to receive any more books, I can return the shipping statement marked "cancel." If I don't cancel, I will receive 6 brand-new novels every month and be billed just $4.24 per book in the U.S. or $4.99 per book in Canada. That's a saving of at least 15% off the cover price! It's quite a bargain! Shipping and handling is just 50¢ per book in the U.S. and 75¢ per book in Canada.* I understand that accepting the 2 free books and gifts places me under no obligation to buy anything. I can always return a shipment and cancel at any time. Even if I never buy another book, the two free books and gifts are mine to keep forever.

235/335 SDN FC7H

Name	(PLEASE PRINT)

Address		Apt. #

City	State/Prov.	Zip/Postal Code

Signature (if under 18, a parent or guardian must sign)

Mail to the Reader Service:
IN U.S.A.: P.O. Box 1867, Buffalo, NY 14240-1867
IN CANADA: P.O. Box 609, Fort Erie, Ontario L2A 5X3

Not valid for current subscribers to Silhouette Special Edition books.

Want to try two free books from another line?
Call 1-800-873-8635 or visit www.ReaderService.com.

* Terms and prices subject to change without notice. Prices do not include applicable taxes. Sales tax applicable in N.Y. Canadian residents will be charged applicable taxes. Offer not valid in Quebec. This offer is limited to one order per household. All orders subject to credit approval. Credit or debit balances in a customer's account(s) may be offset by any other outstanding balance owed by or to the customer. Please allow 4 to 6 weeks for delivery. Offer available while quantities last.

Your Privacy—The Reader Service is committed to protecting your privacy. Our Privacy Policy is available online at www.ReaderService.com or upon request from the Reader Service.

We make a portion of our mailing list available to reputable third parties that offer products we believe may interest you. If you prefer that we not exchange your name with third parties, or if you wish to clarify or modify your communication preferences, please visit us at www.ReaderService.com/consumerschoice or write to us at Reader Service Preference Service, P.O. Box 9062, Buffalo, NY 14269. Include your complete name and address.

USA TODAY *bestselling author Lynne Graham*
is back with a thrilling new trilogy
SECRETLY PREGNANT, CONVENIENTLY WED

Three heroines must marry alpha males to keep
their dreams...but Alejandro, Angelo and Cesario
are not about to be tamed!

Book 1—JEMIMA'S SECRET
Available March 2011 from Harlequin Presents®.

JEMIMA yanked open a drawer in the sideboard to find Alfie's birth certificate. Her son was her husband's child. It was a question of telling the truth whether she liked it or not. She extended the certificate to Alejandro.

"This has to be nonsense," Alejandro asserted.

"Well, if you can find some other way of explaining how I managed to give birth by that date and Alfie not be yours, I'd like to hear it," Jemima challenged.

Alejandro glanced up, golden eyes bright as blades and as dangerous. "All this proves is that you must still have been pregnant when you walked out on our marriage. It does not automatically follow that the child is mine."

"'I know it doesn't suit you to hear this news now and I really didn't want to tell you. But I can't lie to you about it. Someday Alfie may want to look you up and get acquainted."

"If what you have just told me is the truth, if that little boy does prove to be mine, it was vindictive and extremely selfish of you to leave me in ignorance!"

Jemima paled. "When I left you, I had no idea that I was still pregnant."

"Two years is a long period of time, yet you made no attempt to inform me that I might be a father. I will want DNA tests to confirm your claim before I make any decision about what I want to do."

"Do as you like," she told him curtly. "*I* know who Alfie's father is and there has never been any doubt of his identity."

"I will make arrangements for the tests to be carried out and I will see you again when the result is available," Alejandro drawled with lashings of dark Spanish masculine reserve.

"I'll contact a solicitor and start the divorce," Jemima proffered in turn.

Alejandro's eyes narrowed in a piercing scrutiny that made her uncomfortable. "It would be foolish to do anything before we have that DNA result."

"I disagree," Jemima flashed back. "I should have applied for a divorce the minute I left you!"

Alejandro quirked an ebony brow. "And why didn't you?"

Jemima dealt him a fulminating glance but said nothing, merely moving past him to open her front door in a blunt invitation for him to leave.

"I'll be in touch," he delivered on the doorstep.

What is Alejandro's next move? Perhaps rekindling their marriage is the only solution! But will Jemima agree?

*Find out in Lynne Graham's
exciting new romance
JEMIMA'S SECRET*

*Available March 2011
from Harlequin Presents®.*

Copyright © 2011 by Lynne Graham

HPEXP0311

Start your Best Body today with these top 3 nutrition tips!

1. SHOP THE PERIMETER OF THE GROCERY STORE: The good stuff—fruits, veggies, lean proteins and dairy—always line the outer edges of the store. When you veer into the center aisles, you enter the temptation zone, where the unhealthy foods live.

2. WATCH PORTION SIZES: Most portion sizes in restaurants are nearly twice the size of a true serving and at home, it's easy to "clean your plate." Use these easy serving guidelines:
- Protein: the palm of your hand
- Grains or Fruit: a cup of your hand
- Veggies: the palm of two open hands

3. USE THE RAINBOW RULE FOR PRODUCE: Your produce drawers should be filled with every color of fruits and vegetables. The greater the variety, the more vitamins and other nutrients you add to your diet.

Find these and many more helpful tips in

YOUR BEST BODY NOW
by
TOSCA RENO
WITH STACY BAKER

Bestselling Author of
THE EAT-CLEAN DIET®

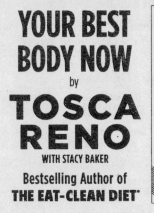

Available wherever books are sold!

NTRSERIESFEB